T0065264

WAR
IN THE TIME OF PR

WAR
IN THE TIME OF PR

J.F. CRONIN

WAR IN THE TIME OF PR

iUniverse books may be ordered through booksellers or by contacting:

iUniverse
1663 Liberty Drive
Bloomington, IN 47403
www.iuniverse.com
844-349-9409

ISBN: 978-1-6632-1001-2 (sc)
ISBN: 978-1-6632-1002-9 (e)

Library of Congress Control Number: 2020918768

Print information available on the last page.

iUniverse rev. date: 11/16/2020

CHAPTER 1

THE GAMBIT

Joshua Ault Bolte was proof that a universally disliked person could rise to a position of power in government. Granted, his wasn't an elected position where he would have had to kiss babies and have people skills. He'd been appointed as the national security adviser because of his purported expertise in world affairs, a reputation gained despite his never having taken interest in other people's cultures or the things that motivated them. He spoke as if he knew about the workings of the world, but he was a charlatan who scratched out a good living by attaching himself to think tanks and working as a television talking head who was rolled out at times of international crisis to spout doomsday predictions. The wilder his worldview became, the more a cult of rabid people followed him. Considered to be an intellectual, he flourished when his associates pushed that idea. Having people who considered him brilliant insulated him, allowing him to communicate with those he considered his intellectual equals. Thinking few were intelligent enough to engage him in conversation, he didn't accommodate other people's ideas. Propped up by like-minded people, he believed the

1

world was a dangerous place that could only be ordered through the use of military force. Famous for predicting an apocalyptic end if the United States were to continue on its present course, he was surrounded by a zealous following of war-firsters. The standing joke summing up his philosophy was that he'd never seen a war he didn't like, and the contested relations between nations could only be solved militarily. In his worldview, there were no allies, and every country was out to get the United States. Scoffing at treaties, he considered them disadvantageous, and he resented that his countrymen weren't remaining vigilant. Therefore, he took it upon himself to try to figure out every country's evil intention toward the United States and the ways to counter it, which always led him to call for the use of military force.

For a supposed expert with a reputation for being a strategic thinker, Bolte often erred in his predictions, but because he was a television personality, no one really cared; his pronouncements were lost in the news cycle. If he had been a baseball player, his percentage of correct predictions, offered in think tanks and on cable news shows, would have been below the Mendoza Line, a batting average of two hundred. His dire worldview was out of touch with reality, but the wilder his pronouncements, the more he was either lauded or berated by people who were in and out of power in Washington. Bolte was either loved or hated. There was no person who didn't have an opinion of him. As the ultimate Manichean thinker, professing that there was only good and evil in the world, black and white, with no shading, Bolte saw enemies lurking who had to be smitten, defeated with military force. His love of using the military to solve political problems was a late-in-life development. As a young man, he could have served in the military and observed the limits of the use of military force close up, but he had bailed on serving in his generation's war.

His desire was to reshape the world into regimes that would be either subservient to the United States or defeated by it. The American firsters loved him and didn't take into account that international friends and enemies were ever changing. Personalizing his worldview, Bolte considered those who didn't agree with him dangerous. He saw himself as the bulwark against them. In his mind, he was a virtuous man isolated because those in government, the people who compromised it, did not approach his philosophical purity. As an outlier, his inclusion in government appeased those who thought like him. His presence quieted fringe elements seeking the next war. Bolte's extreme positions were pointed to by his superiors when they made decisions that weren't radical, making them look sane.

Aware of his reputation, he took satisfaction in being disliked. It made him feel unsoiled by the realities that came with acting as the national security adviser, a position from which he could spout his ideas and few could argue with him, least of all try to convince him of anything other than that which he believed. Having people point out facts that flew in the face of his long-held beliefs merely angered him. Those who worked around him didn't like the maelstrom of tension his snits created.

Bolte's appearance augmented his prickly personality, so it was unknown if people avoided him for his thinking or his looks. He had an oversized, pear-shaped head, inverted on slender shoulders, narrowing down to his chin. Clumps of gray hair flared from his head randomly, seeming to enlarge it, making it look tenuously balanced on his pencil-thin neck. It was difficult to determine the true size of his neck because of the wattles that ran from his chin. In trying to hide his weak chin, he'd grown a bushy beard, but that didn't work; it had only made him look unclean. With so large a head, his eyes were close-set and intense, giving him a feral appearance.

Bolte prided himself not only on his purity of thought but also on his work ethic. He arrived at work precisely at 04:45 each day, before any of his staff, and stayed until at least 18:30, a time well after his staff had departed. No one was sure what he did in the long days, but no one dared ask.

3

At 04:50 he had been seated at his desk for only a few minutes when the phone rang. The only other person who would be up at that time wanting to talk was the president, Wilbur Baron.

"Yes, sir?" Bolte answered the phone.

"I want to talk to you. I'm up. Come over to the residence." The president gave no indication of what he wanted to talk about, but that didn't bother Bolte. He liked the one-on-ones because if he could get a decision out of Baron, then he could run with it and shape it to his liking.

Picking up his cell phone, Bolte walked the empty halls in the Executive Office Building before making the short walk to the White House. Having made the trip many times, he mulled over what Baron might want to talk about. They usually met in the Oval Office. Being invited to the residence at such an early hour was not routine. Bolte assumed the president had an urgent matter that he wanted to discuss and couldn't think of what that might be. Baron was consumed with national politics and was uninformed about the international order. With the president having a political rally the following day, Bolte assumed that he might be asked to discuss an overseas hot spot that might be used to rouse the crowd.

Walking past half-asleep Secret Service personnel, Bolte didn't acknowledge them, but they let him pass.

"He's in the bedroom," an agent outside the door informed him.

Bolte was uncomfortable. He didn't know in what state of dress he might find his boss.

His worst fears were realized when he entered. The president had come out of the shower and had a towel wrapped around his waist. The exposed skin was so white and puffy that it reminded Bolte of the Al Capp cartoon creations, the soft, white, almost shapeless shmoos. He wanted to look away, but being there on business, he had to engage the obese man.

They weren't alone. A hairstylist sprayed the scant hairs on Baron's head individually with some kind of thickening substance

4

that smelled like burnt rubber. When it was applied, the hair could be pushed into position and wouldn't move.

Bolte knew better than to start the conversation. Getting the president's hair positioned was more important than any national security matter, so he sat, disgusted about being a party to the image making that was taking place.

After positioning the hair, the stylist bronzed the president's face and sprayed a perfume to kill the odor of the rubber hair holder and the bronzer. It was an odd color display. Baron's face, neck, and hands, where they would be exposed from under his shirts, were a burnt orange, whereas the rest of his body was as white as baking powder. Where the skin tones blended into one another, the stylist had painted on a clear paint-like substance that, when dry, would prevent the phony tan from bleeding into the white shirts Baron always wore.

Bolte wanted to look away as the stylist's assistant entered the room to help in shaping the president's body. The two men forced Baron's soft skin into a tight T-shirt and started wrapping his body in Saran Wrap. They had given up on getting Baron into a Spanx because none could tighten his lower belly, so he stood erect while the wrap was applied and his flesh was jabbed into the package. As the assistant tightened the wrapping, flesh oozed out, requiring the application of more of the plastic sheeting to pull in the stomach. The wrap was pulled so tight that Baron assumed a forward lean, and when he stood or sat, he had to lean forward. Baron's upper body was packaged into a tight bundle, one that restricted upper-body movement.

The stylist and the body shaper circled the president, with the stylist making a few last swipes with a comb before pronouncing the job perfect. He handed the president a mirror so he could inspect the finished product.

"This better hold. I'll be outdoors today, and it's supposed to be windy."

"It will hold, sir." The stylist excused himself, but the president didn't acknowledge that Bolte was in the room. He turned his attention to a bank of televisions, where programs had been DVR.'ed from the previous evening, to see how the media and late-night comics had treated him. Although he was satisfied that he didn't have to fight any verbal battles with the networks, he wasn't so happy with the comics. "I made that son of a bitch. If it hadn't been for me appearing on his show when he was a nothing, he wouldn't have a job." Baron fumed. "Ungrateful bastard."

Bolte didn't know whom the president was talking about because there was a bank of televisions on.

The president stiffly turned to Bolte. "You've haven't done a thing to get us out of Afghanistan, so I intend to amp up the negotiations by bringing the Taliban negotiators to Camp David to strike a deal. Cutting a deal with the Taliban will make me look good, so I'm going to announce that at my rally tomorrow. One week from today, I'll cut a deal with the Taliban. They'll have to give me what I want because they have already agreed to many of the terms." There was no transition from late-night comedy to real-world problems. Bolte thought Baron suffered from ADHD. There was a lot roiling in his mind at all times, and he seemed to be unable to focus on any one thing for more than a few minutes. "There was another soldier killed yesterday, and it doesn't look like it's going to get better. We have to close Afghanistan down and pull all the troops out." After making the comment, Baron jumped to another topic. "I made a campaign promise that I would get us out of endless wars, so we have to get out of Afghanistan. I'll announce at the rally that I'm going to cut a deal to get us out of Afghanistan. It'll make me look good." He had repeated himself.

"You can't do that, Mr. President." Bolte was careful when refusing to go along with Baron's suggestion.

"Why not? I promised the people I would end this war, and I think the opportunity is before me now. It will rouse the crowd when they hear me say it."

"Mr. President, if you proceed as you're suggesting, you're going to come off looking like a fool." The moment the words cleared Bolte's lips, he knew he had made a mistake. The one thing everyone who worked around Baron knew was that one must say nothing to challenge the president's self-image. To suggest that he might look like a fool crossed all the psychological barriers that kept his ego intact.

Baron reacted to the words as if he had been slapped in the face. He was stunned.

Bolte tried to make up for his mistake by explaining his thinking, but it was futile. The president had receded into his insular world, bothered by the idea that he might look foolish. Bolte had opened that door in Baron's mind, and it unnerved him.

"Mr. President," Bolte spoke as if he were talking to a balky child, "a week from today is the anniversary of the attacks on the Twin Towers and the attacks on the United States. You can't bring in negotiators from a country that housed many of the terrorists and host them at Camp David. That would be sacrilegious and would fly in the face of American values. Shanksville, Pennsylvania, where the fourth plane went down, is only miles from Camp David. It would make you look as if you had forgotten the suffering this country has endured. It's a bad idea." Again, Bolte had overstepped the unwritten rule of refraining from telling the president that one of his ideas was bad. Trying to bring the conversation to a more businesslike footing, Bolte changed the subject.

"I was briefed, as I'm sure you were, that the peace negotiations with the Taliban are proceeding well." A few days earlier, Baron had lauded the progress of the negotiations. Bolte hoped to piggyback on that euphoria.

"That's bullshit. Our guys don't know how to cut a deal, and the Taliban are slow-walking them. They have our guys by the balls and aren't going to give up a thing. Why should they? They are kicking our ass."

"The sticking point is that the Taliban isn't agreeing to enter into a power-sharing agreement with the sitting government."

"And they won't. They want to keep us tied down. They want to bleed us until we pack up and leave." The president paused as if looking for the right words. "I don't care. They can have the place. You told me that if I announce I'm bringing the Taliban to Camp David, I'll look like a fool. Well, give me some solutions. All I get from you is no, no, no. What would you propose to get us out of the war?" Baron shouted at his national security adviser.

Bolte could see that the president couldn't get over the fact that he had suggested that he might look foolish. "You're supposed to be a smart guy, but you don't know shit about cutting deals. So, Mr. Smart Guy, tell me how we get our troops out of Afghanistan quickly. I want all the right things said about how we support the government, but as far as I'm concerned, the Taliban can own the place." Baron stopped and took a heated breath. "Well, do you have any suggestions about how you want to proceed?"

Bolte had never been in a confrontation like this with Baron. He didn't know what to say.

"You come up with a plan and let me see it. If it looks good, we'll run with it." The president, agitated, moved quickly, causing his breasts above the plastic wrap to flop.

Bolte knew he was done as the national security adviser, but he didn't want Baron to have the last word.

"Why don't you have the military stage a battle to draw the Taliban into confronting us and win it with overpowering airpower? By winning a small battle, you could claim total victory over the Taliban and say we have won the larger war. With a victory, you could set the terms you want for leaving the country." It was a throwaway thought so devoid of intellectual rigor that Bolte was ashamed that he had mentioned it, but it was his way of not letting the president get the upper hand.

"That's stupid. We are already in a war with the Taliban." Baron was agitated. "You can leave now. I'll get back to you on this."

⎯⎯⎯

Bolte was glad to leave the meeting, feeling that he was escaping a house that was on fire. He was in favor of letting the peace negotiations continue, knowing that if the Afghan government were sold out, the region would be plunged into chaos, which would eventually result in the reintroduction of US troops. As far as Bolte was concerned, he had been given carte blanche to do an impossible job. He had to develop a plan for an honorable way for the United States to leave the war, but he was pragmatic enough to know there had to be a part of any plan that would shine the light of brilliance on the president. That was the most important part. The outcome didn't matter. The optics were what was important. In the back of his mind, Bolte knew that no matter what he came up with, it wouldn't be enough.

Walking back to his office, Bolte started thinking about how he could get the United States out of Afghanistan without having the entire region crater. He agreed with the president's desire to leave the United States' longest war, but he had his own reasons for it. A troop withdrawal would free up troops to use against Iran, the country Bolte saw as the most imminent threat in the Middle East. Iran was the country he considered the real enemy. With Afghanistan out of the way, he could focus on Iran.

⎯⎯⎯

The president, as he always did after being told he shouldn't do something by his staff, went outside the government to seek the advice of friends. One friend he relied on heavily was Erik King. They had come from similar backgrounds of wealth and privilege, fantasy worlds in which they'd never heard the word *no* and had shared many of the same life experiences. Both had inherited enormous wealth from powerful fathers and had lived their lives in the great men's shadows. Both had been given everything they wanted in life except the thing they desired most, fraternal recognition. Their fathers were busy amassing wealth and didn't have time to take an interest in them. They became part of the financial empires, chattel, made to succeed so as not to besmirch the reputation of their fathers, who had never lost at anything. Being treated as commodities scarred both men emotionally and mentally. It hurt more psychologically when they were shipped off to private schools so their fathers wouldn't have them underfoot. Essentially, their fathers had left them in the care of their mothers, weak women who dared not question anything their husbands ordered. Both sons had come to see their mothers, and women in general, as weak pawns used to prop up men.

Both Baron and King had done well in business, but nothing approximating what their fathers had done. They suffered with the thought that without the boost their fathers had provided, they might not have been able to compete in the real world. The thought that they might actually be inferior was buried in their psyches. To compensate, they had developed outsized personalities so that no one would look too closely at their mental makeup. Their bombast covered up a lot of flaws, and part of the bombast was to look down on anyone who worked for the government. They were considered people who shouldn't be consulted in a time of crisis. Decisions should be made by those who had wealth and could see the big picture.

With an air of superiority, both King and Baron insulated themselves from having to deal with civil servants. Along with several other scions of wealth, they had formed a "big boys' club" on which the president relied to give him advice. Membership into the big boys' club was limited to those who had outsized wealth. But even among the big boys, there was a pecking order based on how long it took each man to write a ten-million-dollar check. King's fortune had come from manufacturing and was grounded in real money, so all knew that he could write the check at any time. Baron had paper wealth, and it took him time to move around assets to write the check. It was a distinction that allowed King to look down on the president, despite the fact that he was the supposedly most powerful man in the world.

King, a professed Libertarian who openly despised big government, had started ISSAC, International Surveillance, Security, and Construction Systems, and, under the banner of security, had amassed a private army, one that he could command once the institutions of government failed and the real patriots took over the country. In the meantime, while awaiting Armageddon, he attached himself to the government he despised and milked every penny out of it. His surveillance services didn't do anything more than the military was already doing, but he used his influence in Congress and elsewhere in Washington to make ISSAC indispensable. Using his money and influence, he inserted ISSAC between defense contractors and the military so that he had outsized influence over the military's drone programs. His surveillance operations had contractors working side by side with the military. Realizing the military changed out personnel every two or three years, his long-term employees had become the experts in the field and were now indispensable to the drone programs. Understanding that that wasn't where the money was to be made, King had partnered with defense contractors to write up specifications for drones and then had turned around and sold them to the military. He had his hands into so many agencies that, in addition to having built a private army to protect against end times, he essentially had a shadow government.

"Erik." The president treated him like he treated no one else on his staff. "Hey. I've got the solution to a problem that the whiz kids around here say can't be implemented. I want to run it by you to hear what you think."

"If you want my advice, are you going to pay me some of the big bucks you pay those dolts?"

"I'll take you golfing."

"You know I'm always at your service, Wil." He had shortened the name Wilbur, realizing the president didn't like it. It was a soft name. No other person in or out of government could get by using the president's first name, but that didn't stop King. They were like brothers.

"Here's where I'm running into resistance from the dolts. I think it would be a great idea to end the war in Afghanistan with a big PR rollout. What I wanted to do, since the negotiations are almost settled, was to bring the Taliban negotiators to Camp David to close the deal, where I'd have a big signing and make it a press event."

King stopped listening. The security arm of ISSAC had almost half a billion dollars in contracts in effect in Afghanistan. Once the war was closed down, that money might be cut off. He wasn't going to let the war end quickly if he could prevent it, but he had no idea how to temper the advice he would give to the president. Searching for an answer that would be good for business while trying to accommodate the president's wishes, he stalled. "Why do the whiz kids object to that?" He was hoping that by piggybacking on what the president's staff might have told him, he could retain the president's friendship and continue the war.

"They made up some phony reason that bringing the Taliban to Camp David on the anniversary of 9/11 might turn into a press disaster."

The words were enough to give King an idea of the resistance the president was facing.

"Wil, I know that the slugs who work for you can't get out of their own way, but that bit of advice may be worth listening to. The optics would be bad, and you know, the fake news would blow your actions out of proportion." King thought his words might stop the president's rash act, but he immediately thought of how any action to stop the war in Afghanistan was going to affect ISSAC. There was a lot of money involved with anything the president did. "Mr. President, you're the ultimate dealmaker. Why don't you stage a PR coup and announce that you are getting involved in the negotiations? With your dealmaking skills, you could break any tie between our side and the Taliban." As King said it, he knew his suggestion was impossible. If the president were to get involved, it would slow the process to a crawl because Baron wouldn't be able to focus on the task.

"You're telling me the optics of a Camp David summit would be terrible?"

"Wil, the press would raise holy hell, and it might cost you some votes."

"Erik, that's why I call you. You always provide me with good advice. I think I'll cancel plans for Camp David, and maybe I'll take a look at the negotiating. What I'll do is make a statement that the negotiations are continuing." Baron lingered on that thought for a moment. "I'll call you tomorrow. We'll try to get a golf game in."

"Yes, sir."

―――――

By the time he got to his office, Bolte, thinking about his encounter with the president, smiled. He was embarrassed that he had thrown out the idea of starting a deflective war that could be won and whose victory could be spread over the entire conflict. He realized it was a crazy idea when he'd mentioned it and was glad that Baron had shot it down, but he was convinced the rejection was the result of a snit over his broaching the idea that the president might look like a fool. No matter what he had proposed, it would have been turned down. Such was always the case when the president was trying to protect his image. Whatever the reason, Bolte was glad Baron hadn't listened to him. Sitting at his desk, he knew he had opened a window in Baron's mind that would further dampen an already cold relationship. He was convinced he couldn't work for Baron any longer. With that realization, Bolte started penciling notes for a resignation letter. When his ideas were on paper, he read them over and thought they conveyed the things that he wanted to say. Knowing it would be unfair to dump his resignation on Baron without forewarning, he picked up the phone and called him.

"Mr. President, this is Josh Bolte. Have you got a few minutes to chat?"

"Yeah. What do you want?" There was no friendliness.

"I've been thinking that after our conversation earlier this morning, I'm not serving you well. I think you need someone in this job who thinks along the lines that fit into your worldview. That said, I'm going to send my letter of resignation over to your office. Even with our differences, it has been an honor to have worked with you." Bolte was soft selling. Working for Baron had been a nightmare.

"Josh, don't be too hasty. Take some time to think about it. We'll talk about it in a couple of days."

The president asking for a delay stunned Bolte. He thought Baron would have been happy to get rid of him. "Whatever you wish, sir." Bolte hung up, confused.

The confusion lasted only forty-five minutes. His secretary came into his office to inform him he had been fired.

He couldn't believe it. Only minutes earlier he had told the president that he would hold off sending his resignation letter over to the White House. He had no choice but to believe he was without a job as his secretary showed him the president's tweet. Bolte thought the tweet went to the heart of Baron's dishonesty.

CHAPTER 2

THE PAWNS

The president, faced with having to choose a new national security adviser, was determined not to make the same mistake he had made with the previous two. He wasn't going to select someone who had their own ideas about how the national security apparatus should be run. He wanted someone who had no preconceived ideas on how the country should interface with the world, a person who would fall in line behind him, come hell or high water. He had his staff search for possible candidates. After a frantic two days of culling the hundreds of people recommended to them, they had narrowed the field down to two. The president would make the final decision.

He settled on Stanley Weeks, for all the wrong reasons. Weeks had worked in and around national security and Washington for years, but in all that time he had been a second banana. He had attached himself to the system, bounding from one job to the next without ever rising to the tier of top-level thinkers. He was known in conservative circles because he was a joiner, a person who attached himself to groups spouting conservative ideology and pushing their views. Weeks was known for accepting ideas of others without question. As the ultimate hanger-on, never doing enough to get noticed, never doing too little to get fired, he was a yes-man who had been recommended to the president by a congressman who attended many of the same meetings as Weeks. Weeks did have attributes that Baron placed a lot of emphasis on. Weeks was telegenic with silver hair neatly cut. He was as tall as the president but was very trim. His deep-set eyes gave him an air of seriousness, and that translated well on television. Unlike Bolte, with whom Baron was seldom photographed, Weeks was the type of man the president wanted in the photos with him when he discussed national security matters. Weeks would not be asked for his advice but would serve as a handsome potted plant to make the president look as if he had competent advisers.

Baron evaluated his choice in their first meeting.

Weeks sat across the desk from him. The president's special advisers sat in overstuffed chairs along the walls.

"Stanley, I have to get us out of Afghanistan. I want you to make that a priority."

"Yes, sir." Weeks was excited to please.

"If we continue to negotiate, the war is going to go on, for how long no one knows. Have you got any ideas on how to get us out of the war?"

"I haven't thought about it, but give me some time and I'll have an answer for you."

"Yeah." The president showed his dissatisfaction with the answer. Weeks squirmed.

"I have an idea that may work." Baron paused to be sure Weeks was listening. "Wars end with battles in which victory can be declared, and I want a victory. I was thinking, we could bomb Afghanistan into oblivion. We have that power, but we just can't bomb indiscriminately. We need a reason. We have to entice the Taliban into taking a risk and trying to take on one of our ground units. When they do, we can bomb them into submission, declare victory, and end the war any way we want to."

"That's a good idea, Mr. President," Weeks responded before even thinking about the problem.

The thoughtless approval of his unformulated plan pleased Baron, making him happy. He had the thought that the new national security adviser was going to be a good team member. "As I see it, you can plan something like this in-house, where you won't have to inform the military or any of the other agencies. My idea is to use only the assets we presently have on the ground. So if you come up with a plan, I'll approve it, and no one will be able to bitch."

"I'll get my staff on it immediately."

"I knew I could count on you." Baron dismissed Weeks disdainfully.

It was early in the morning. The people whom Weeks was going to assign to work the project weren't yet in their offices. He was going to keep the planning group small because he hadn't been in office long enough to know who on the staff he had inherited could be trusted to carry out the president's ideas without leaking them to the press. Having worked with two people he felt safe entrusting such an important job to, he would assign them to the project, which would be code-named Angel Fire.

Abby Dunne wasn't new to the Washington world of national security chitchat. She was a Swarthmore graduate who had served as an assistant editor for a political publication that critiqued national security. She had met Weeks years prior at a conference, where she had interviewed him. He considered her smart, but more than that, she had a face that always drew second glances. He was loath to admit it, but he shared some of the same vanity as Baron. He liked being around attractive people, having convinced himself that they were better workers. With Abby's looks, he ascribed intelligence and diligence to her without ever having seen a meaningful work product. Almost six feet tall, she was crowned with shoulder-length blonde hair, sapphire-blue eyes, and plump red lips that were colored without the aid of lipstick. The lips separated when she smiled, showing off perfectly white teeth. After meeting her the first time,

Weeks had kept her business card. As the national security adviser, with the ability to hire his own staff, he made her his first choice.

The second member of the team was Barry Waddle. Barry had survived much the same way Weeks had. He attended the same meetings and was a hanger-on in Washington without ever having been acknowledged for his work in the national security establishment. He was a survivor who moved from job to job in government unnoticed. He and Weeks had worked low-level projects together. Weeks liked the way he fell into line without questioning, but more than that, he knew he would be trusted as a team player.

Timing was important. Weeks felt that he had to get a plan to the president quickly so that he could show Baron he had made the right choice in selecting him. He wanted a full plan, something he could present to Baron without the usual interagency staffing that bogged down so many things in Washington. Acting at the president's direction, he could avoid the interagency squabbles that would surely accompany getting any plan approved through normal channels.

When the staff came to work, the first message on the computers of two trusted aides was that they were to attend a meeting at 09:15. The timing of the meeting indicated something had come up that they had not been aware of the day before.

"Okay, here's the problem," Weeks started before Dunne and Waddle could get seated. "The president has the idea that we are never going to get out of Afghanistan via the peace negotiations that are dragging on. He wants to get out without making it look like we are being chased out. He wants us to come up with a plan that will allow us to make an honorable exit from the war and from Afghanistan itself. His idea is that we need a fight there that we can win, because he feels wars can only be won if there is something on which to tie a victory. He wants to draw the Taliban into a fight, decisively defeat them, declare victory, and leave. The problem, as I see it, is that if this is done too precipitously, the Afghan government will fall, which is something the president doesn't seem to care about.

So we can't get bogged down worrying about second- and third-level effects. Our job is to solve the single problem with no consideration given to the after-mess. For now, treat it that way. Who knows, tomorrow the president might be high on negotiations again." Weeks spoke without parsing his words because he really didn't know what Baron wanted. "I'd like to give you more to work with, but you have everything the president told me. Based on the limited information I've given you, do any of you have any ideas that I can run by the president in the event that he calls?" Weeks threw the meeting open to his subordinates.

Both members of the selected team looked dumbfounded. Abby, who was supposed to be a first-class thinker, felt compelled to say something. Being new to the ways of the National Security Council (NSC), she didn't hesitate to offer her ideas, thinking she was the brightest bulb in the room. "We are always fighting the Taliban, but our engagements with them don't rise to the level of a pitched battle. With negotiations going off and on, the military is reluctant to go out and look for a fight that might rise to the level that might arouse the public's interest. It's like they are in survival mode, unwilling to lose personnel in what they see as a lost cause."

"That attitude doesn't rise to the level of the president's expectations." Weeks stopped her. "We need a battle that will allow the president to bask in the favorable press coverage that we could generate, so then he could take credit for winning the final battle of the United States' longest war."

"What happens to the Afghan government?" Waddle was playing devil's advocate, suggesting there were no easy answers and that any course of action had to be thought through more fully, despite the fact Weeks had told them not to think ahead.

"That's the challenge. We have to dump the Afghan government without giving the appearance that we are dumping them." Weeks was thinking aloud. "No matter what's decided, we have to put a complementary strategy in place that will make the president look good. I'm not talking about a quick shot that will only dominate one news cycle; we have to make him look like a commander in chief and show that he is a hands-on leader. We have to have cameras and story lines in place for every action taken in Afghanistan."

The group fell silent.

"We have almost ten thousand security contractors running around Afghanistan, and no one knows what they are doing because they all work for different agencies. How about if we fight a battle as you suggest and then we backfill the military manpower we will extract out of Afghanistan with contractors and thereby privatize the war? The president has floated that idea several times. He could take credit for ending the war and propping up the government. It would be a win-win." Barry was almost surprised to hear his voice; he couldn't believe what he had suggested.

"What about the costs?" Weeks asked. "Contractors are expensive."

"No matter how many of them are used, Congress will approve the money for them. We have about twelve thousand in Iraq, and no one has batted an eye. Privatization of the military is a sellable idea in Congress because everyone makes money."

Weeks had heard enough. "Okay, drop everything you're doing and put your heads together to see what you can come up with. We'll meet at 17:30 to determine what, if anything, works."

"We've spent the last couple of years signaling that we wouldn't abandon the Afghan government. Can we assume that is out the window?" Abby had heard Weeks say that it was, but she wanted reinforcement so that the planning would not go crosswise to reality.

"Regardless how we leave Afghanistan, their government is fucked, so don't let saving it bother you. I think upping the numbers of contractors will allow us to appease the Afghan government. If not, who gives a shit? They're screwed no matter what happens after the military leaves." Weeks was curt.

"Is it on that assumption that you want us to proceed?" She wanted clarification.

"Yes." Weeks was thinking how such a charade could be made to work.

"The Taliban fight how they want, when they want, so getting them on the battlefield in a large-scale offensive will be nearly impossible, especially since they feel they are winning. With that mindset, they wouldn't engage our forces in a fixed-piece battle. And if they did, there would be American and Taliban casualties." Waddle gave his opinion.

"You sound like the goddamn military. They've been dragging their feet in hunting down the Taliban because they don't want to take casualties. Forget casualties. Don't treat this as a cost-benefit analysis. Give me some ideas devoid of the costs, devoid of reality if you will." Weeks was trying to overcome the reluctance of his team to provide him with ideas that hadn't already been shot down by the military. "If there is a way to get the Taliban into a fight, I want you to find it." The Afghanistan piece was just a small part of his worldview, but he could see good things happening if he could find a way to get out of Afghanistan. "I want some workable ideas by the end of the day." He dismissed his staffers and then informed his secretary to clear his schedule. He needed time to think about what he wanted to do.

The afternoon meeting was conducted after normal working hours. Dunne and Waddle sat down at Weeks's conference table and unrolled a map of Afghanistan. Weeks looked at it and seemed disinterested.

Abby was chosen as the spokesman. "We worked all the angles on this, and the data we have indicates that the only time the Taliban have to come at us directly is when we have interfered with their drug operations."

"What are you thinking?" Weeks asked.

"There are two places where they have fought us every time we have tried to control the ground: the times we have moved forces into the Korangal Valley to block their infiltration and supply routes, and in the Zukan Valley, the hub of their drug-trafficking operation.

They don't want us in the Zukan Valley. They get us to leave by making us pay a steep price in casualties. The military can see no strategic value in fighting for the valley, so they have ceded it to the Taliban."

"What do you think?" Weeks asked Waddle.

"I think the Korangal is a nonstarter. They don't infiltrate as many fighters as they used to, so that valley has lost some of its significance. There is no guarantee that the Taliban would fight for it today as they have in the past. That said, it's remote, and supporting operations there has always been difficult. The military has avoided it for those reasons. The Zukan Valley seems like the more logical place. It is closer to all our central support bases, and it has road networks, which we have built, tying it to the rest of the country. Its economy is built on the drug trade. The Taliban grow the poppies, process it into opium, and transport it to wherever they can make the most money. It's a soup to nuts drug operation. Anytime we have tried to interfere with their business, soldiers get killed and the military ceases operations. We essentially know what's going on with the drugs, and we continue to condone it. I think if were looking for a fight, we could find it in the Zukan Valley."

Weeks liked the way the conversation was going.

"The military wouldn't buy into going back into Zukan Valley. They'd raise hell about the casualties they would take," Abby offered.

"Goddamn military. We pay them to fight, and they run around finding excuses to avoid getting bloody. Well, I have no such compunction. The big picture is much more important than a few dead bodies." Weeks showed his cold, unthinking side.

"A second option," Abby Dunne added, "is to declare the truce talks a success and pull all the troops out, then backfill immediately with civilian contractors. That would save a battle and essentially garner the same results. We'd continue to prop up the Afghan government as we have been."

Weeks frowned, shutting down the suggestion. "The president would never buy into that. He's a big-splash guy. He wants a victory that he could take credit for. He would buy into a battle that he could say he approved and led, but he would be reluctant to leave Afghanistan through the truce talks. He might be criticized. I realize the results would be the same, but the optics are off. That's what's important. We have to make him look like a strong leader. If we do that, any plan we send over to the White House will be approved. Then we could be out of Afghanistan in a month." Weeks pushed his chair away from the table and leaned back. He liked the idea of a battle against the Afghan drug trade. He had heard Baron mention the United States' inability to cut it off. The proposal before him would be a double win for him with the president.

"Another option," Dunne continued, "is to increase troop strength once again and blanket Kandahar Province, driving the Taliban off the land, then pull our troops out before they can reestablish themselves."

"That's dead in the water," Weeks said, stopping her. "More troops to Afghanistan would never be approved. Let's think about the Zukan idea."

"It's what we kind of agreed on," Waddle started. "It could be accomplished without bringing any additional assets into the country. Everything we need is already there, but it will require the president telling the military how he wants to use those assets."

"I don't see that as a problem," Weeks assured.

"As we see it, if anything less than a company of ground troops were to be inserted into the Zukan Valley to disrupt the drug enterprise, the Taliban would attack to get them out. A unit of a size that could easily be overrun works because there isn't enough force associated with it to shut down the drug operation, but it would be large enough to disrupt it. It's felt that this would draw the Taliban into a fight and, more importantly, inflict American casualties, which would raise calls for us to take strong action. Those actions would be that every air asset in Afghanistan could be used to pound the Taliban into oblivion. It would be an air show unlike any seen in Afghanistan, and regardless of its results, it would allow us to claim victory. The air show would be all that the public would be interested in, so then we could fabricate any story we wanted. We could claim that the Taliban was no longer a creditable fighting force and therefore was no longer a threat to the government. We could pull our troops out under the guise that the war has been won. The president could take his bow, and the United States could get out of the mess it created." Waddle was sure he had the solution.

The advantage, as Weeks saw it, was that he wouldn't have to listen to the military. Everything needed was already in the war zone. All that was required now was to move forces around.

"Work this as an air show. Come up with the fewest number of troops on the ground that would bait the Taliban. The fewer, the better. Then settle on the number of US casualties that would be sufficient for us to unleash an air war. Then come up with a list of aircraft that will be available and sequence how we want to use them. Pick targets that will make a big splash. That might be tricky. Put together a plan that the air force can't shoot down even if they insist on controlling all the airplanes." Weeks grew reflective. The first significant action he was planning was nothing more than shilling for the president. "As you refine the plan, don't forget the PR strategy. Lay it on thick—the thicker, the better. You can envision the desired ending, but build in a moment where the president can be seen in the Situation Room among his advisers calling the shots. Make him look presidential, and then have reams of news releases touting how his plan won the United States' longest war." Weeks didn't like being a pitchman. He got back into character. "I have a meeting with the president in three days. I'll need a plan that I can sell. Once the president buys in, no one will be able to sidetrack this." He dismissed Dunne and Waddle.

Weeks felt good preparing for the meeting where none of those in attendance knew what the president had requested him to do. He and his team had worked out a final solution for Afghanistan that no one else in government was aware of. That gave him an advantage. Everyone would have to respond to him, and he could therefore control the discussion. He was playing over in his mind the points he was going to make, when his secretary opened the door to his office timidly.

"The chief of staff just called and said you are among the chosen today." The secretary entered the office and nervously gave him his orders. Being one of the chosen meant that he was one of the people who would be meeting with the president who would have to compliment him before giving his presentation. At earlier meetings, everyone was required to lavish the president with praise, but that was too time-consuming, so the list had been whittled down to a chosen three.

It was unwelcome news.

"Did the chief of staff give you any indication as to what we should compliment him on today? Any hot-button topics that will make him happy?" Weeks's face tightened. The games the staff played to stroke Baron's ego were shameful, but Weeks, now one of the chosen, would fall into line.

The secretary left him alone. He backed away from his desk and stood, thinking that he wanted to deal with big ideas in solving the problems facing the world. He didn't like being reduced to preschool ego stroking. He submitted to the humiliation because by sitting near the seat of power, he felt he might make a difference. He would have balked, but he was going to be given the opportunity to present a plan that would change the strategic trajectory of the war. He rationalized that a little humiliation was worth it. Drawing himself erect, he resolved to read the comments of praise his secretary had written to inflate the president's ego.

Being the first to arrive at the meeting, Weeks was accompanied by Abby Dunne. She wore a white tailored suit with a low neckline and was too stunning to be ignored. Young and old men fawned over her. Weeks had made the right decision in bringing her along.

She took the spotlight off him and allowed him to get through the small talk with other attendees without being asked any difficult questions. Once he'd taken his seat at the long table behind his name card, Abby sat directly in back of him. As principals of other departments and agencies arrived, they kept their distance. Weeks was viewed with suspicion. They had received word that he was working on a special project for the president, and they didn't like the secrecy.

Prior to the president's arrival, everyone was in their seats. Those next to Weeks found conversation partners away from him. For a man who prided himself on being able to work with everyone, he didn't like the feeling of isolation.

"Ladies and gentlemen, the president of the greatest nation in the world and commander in chief of the greatest fighting force in history." The words announced the president, but it was a moment before he entered, followed by his special advisers.

Although Weeks was among the chosen to laud the president, those in attendance couldn't resist the opportunity to curry favor. They lavished Baron with praise. Weeks couldn't believe that the people essentially running the world were so spineless. There wasn't a one he thought who would voice an opinion other than that which would please the president. Basking in his moral superiority, Weeks, when it came his turn to lavish praise, was ready.

"Mr. President, under your tutelage, we have seen great strides made in changing the world. It is a much safer place than it was when you inherited it from the previous administration." Referring to the previous administration was a twist that Weeks added, knowing the president was obsessed with his predecessor and that he loved to hear he was better. It was a cheap con, but it worked.

The meeting started. Each person at the table discussed what they were working on and how the president might help them overcome obstacles. When it was Weeks's turn, he started slowly

"Mr. President, as we discussed previously, your plan to extricate us from Afghanistan"—he gave the president credit, another cheap ploy to settle an erratic man—"is in the final stages. However, I can give you an overview today so that others can provide input."

Those at the meeting had no idea what Weeks was talking about. It was the first time they had heard the president had a plan to leave Afghanistan. As far as they knew, the peace talks were the plan.

"Hold what you have until after the meeting. You can brief me personally in the Oval Office."

Weeks was delighted. If he could sell the president on his proposal, he could overcome the objections of other agencies, particularly the military, whose resistance he expected.

The meeting ended quickly as Baron was losing interest. When the attendees were finally dismissed, Weeks and Dunne stayed in the conference room, giving the president some time before finally going to the Oval Office. As others departed, the official White House photographer was packing up his gear. Abby Dunne had an idea.

"Have you got some time for a quick project." She engaged the photographer.

"I have nothing scheduled until three this afternoon."

"Can you come with us to the Oval Office?"

"What have you got planned?" Weeks was curious.

"Phase one of the PR campaign." She was smug.

Turning to the photographer, she said, "Come with us as we brief the president. I'm going to be opening a map on his desk. As we look at it, I'd like you to photograph the sequence. Can you do that?"

"That will be easy."

They left the meeting room together.

As they arrived at the Oval Office, they found the president seated at his desk with a dour expression, indicating his reluctance to receive another brief, even one that he had requested. Seeing the photographer seemed to brighten his mood. He smiled as if he had just heard the word *cheese*.

"I hope you don't mind, sir, but I asked Peter"—Weeks was referring to the photographer—"to take a series of shots showing you receiving this first brief. The idea is to show the world that you were involved in the process from start to finish. Then when the mission is complete, you can take full credit."

"Good idea. I like it." The president paused, thinking over how he could bias the coverage. "Who are you?" Baron asked.

"I'm Abby Dunne, one of Mr. Weeks's assistants and a principal in devising the plan we are going to brief."

Baron wasn't listening. In his mind he was staging how he wanted Weeks and Dunne positioned as they briefed him. He especially wanted to get Abby in the photos. Having such a beautiful woman shown briefing him would make him look good. It was the Fox news angle, having all their female talking heads be blonde and beautiful.

"Do you remember the war room where the president sat with his advisers when bin Laden was taken down? I liked that. Could we get something similar?" Baron asked.

"That shouldn't be a problem." Weeks was enthused, liking the genius of what Abby had accomplished. Photos were taken. Baron requested the proofs before they were released. He would pick out the ones that made him look good.

Weeks, walking to the side of the desk where the president was sitting, unfurled a map. "Get a shot of this," he instructed the photographer. With the photos accomplished, he started. "We have determined that the only thing the Taliban will make a stand for is their drug trade. Each time in the past dozen years we have impeded their ability to move drugs through the Zukan Valley, they have fought us. We're pretty sure that if we place a force in the valley, the Taliban will try to oust it. So, we intend to move a small force already in-country into the valley to impede the drug traffic. We expect that this will draw the Taliban into a fight. When they expose themselves, we will use all the air assets in-country to destroy them, also destroying the drug trade. The air war will destroy everything related to drugs. Once that is accomplished, you can form the narrative anyway you like and say the country is stable enough, with the Taliban damaged, for the Afghan government to take control. We would be able to leave Afghanistan declaring a peace. You will be the US president who orchestrated the final battle that ended our longest war and the president who ended the vile drug trade."

"I like it." There were no questions about casualties or what the order of battle might be. The president was consumed with the idea that he might come off looking like a war hero.

The plan, as much of it as they had briefed, was accepted without questions. Weeks understood that he could have briefed that pink monkeys were going to do the fighting, and as long as the pictures were good, Baron would have bought it.

"Mr. President, I think there is an opportunity in what we are trying to do to make you look like a powerful commander in chief, as well as a humanitarian." Abby Dunne was rolling up her maps. Her words caught Weeks by surprise.

"How do you propose to do that?" Baron showed interest.

"While we are photographing you in the Situation Room controlling forces, we will stage an event that will provide you with an opportunity to show your human side. I have looked at a lot of gun camera footage, and I think I've found a clip that we can use to make you look like a peaceful warrior."

"What are you getting at?" Baron remained interested.

"The clip I'd like to use is from Iraq, but it can be spliced in to make it look as it if were actually happening while you are directing aircraft from the Situation Room. It shows people running into a building. We could call it a school. With the gun camera targeting children running into what we'll call a school, you could intercede and call off the plane designated to attack and direct it to another target, while explaining to those gathered with you that you don't want to harm the children. It would play well, allowing the world to see you in a different, gentler light." Abby, not knowing if she had gone too far, stopped abruptly.

Weeks didn't say anything, hoping to take his direction from the president's actions. If Abby's idea was shot down, he would distance himself from it. If, on the other hand, Baron bought in, then he would take the credit.

"I like it. Be sure that is worked in somehow." Baron gave his smiling approval. "You've got a winner here, Stanley. You'd better keep her." He dismissed them.

Walking back to the Executive Office Building, Weeks thought that Abby had one-upped him. He would have to keep an eye on her ambitions.

"We've tried that before." The chairman of the Joint Chiefs cut off Weeks as he discussed his plan with the service chiefs. "The Taliban will come out and fight, but we will take heavy casualties. The last time something like this was tried, we took thirty-nine KIA and about sixty WIA."

"I understand." Weeks didn't let the interruption faze him. "But this will be different. The troops we put in the valley will be placed there as a lure. We will let the Taliban come to them, and when they do, we will blow them into oblivion." Weeks felt that he hadn't convinced the military leaders, so he continued selling the plan. "The advantage of what we are trying to do is that not one extra troop will have to be deployed. All the assets are on the ground in Afghanistan. They merely have to be moved around. Airpower will win this battle. And the air show can be aired on TV, showing all the bells and whistles of the fabulous war machine the president has built. We can include shots of him making important decisions. That will play well."

Hearing of the PR plans and the treatment the president was going to receive, the military leaders realized they would have no say in fighting this part of the war, but still they felt they had to advise against it.

The Central Command commander, who had overall responsibility for the war, looked worried. "This is crazy. We've been in negotiations to get out of Afghanistan, and we keep telling the public the talks are going well. Now, we pull a switch by putting US troops in one of the most treacherous places in the country, which is sure to result in casualties. I don't get it. What are we trying to achieve?"

"We are trying to set up an exit strategy," Weeks answered. "The peace talks aren't going to get us out of Afghanistan with favorable terms. At the rate they are going, we'll be tied down in Afghanistan for another twenty years. The president wants us out of Afghanistan. We have spent a lot of time and money trying to fix a broken government, and it's time to let them stand on their own." Weeks paused to gather his thoughts. "This is an exit strategy, and to achieve an exit, we have to let the pieces fall where they may. If we put on the right show and declare victory, we will be able to walk out of Afghanistan with our heads held high. A victory, even a sham victory, would be the ultimate prize of this war, and with it the president can claim it as his own." He paused, thinking of how he could best close the deal with the Joint Chiefs. "I can tell you that the president has determined that this plan will go forward. It's going to happen. I'd advise each of you to take your piece and run with it. Your objections will be considered, but arguing too strenuously against this plan that the president conceived will be considered disobeying orders—and you know the president will never tolerate that."

With those words, the military leaders knew there was no objecting to what Weeks was proposing. He had boxed them into compliance.

Stanley Weeks was shaking his head as he left the meeting. The one thing he was sure of was that he was going to get the United States out of Afghanistan. He used the KISS method, "Keep it simple, stupid," with the president. The foreboding he had was that Baron hadn't formally approved the proposed actions the United States was about to take and at any moment might change his mind. There was always the danger that the military might get to him and shift his thinking. Weeks wasn't worried about other objections from other agencies because the plan was classified to the point that they hadn't been read into it. The top secret classification prevented leaks and would keep the number of those who knew of what was about to happen to a minimum.

Weeks felt that once the State Department learned what was afoot, they would fight him as they were the ones with oversight of the peace talks. Their job was to talk and talk. The president didn't think that way, but word was leaking out that he had been talking to civilian contractors, causing rumors to abound. The hearsay was that Baron had been working back channels with the Afghan government, in which both sides seemed amenable, to replace the military with civilian contractors. The net result would be no reduction in the number of personnel remaining in the country, but the presence of contractors could be hidden from the American public. The Afghans liked the idea because it would allow them to say they had thrown off the yoke of American colonialism, represented by the military, while also allowing them to hide their dependence on US support. Weeks could only hope that, as with so many previous near misses to a negotiated settlement, the rumor of transferring personnel would fall apart. He felt his hook in Baron were the bells and whistles associated with a grand battle, a made-for-TV battle, in which the United States would inflict a resounding defeat on the Taliban, providing the United States with sufficient cover to leave Afghanistan. The imagery of the president riding down Constitution Avenue in an open-top car, like Caesar returning victorious from Gaul, riding in his chariot, was imagery the president would not replicate at the bargaining table.

Weeks had been working with Dunne and Waddle in finalizing plans and writing orders to direct the military, when his assistant popped his head in the door.

"You'd better turn on the TV."

Weeks didn't like the tone. It sounded ominous. The gathered staff all paid attention to the president's image, which appeared on the screen. He had just authorized another round of peace talks.

Weeks was unhappy with the announcement. He didn't want anything getting in the way of the battle his staff was planning. Listening to the president, he didn't hear anything about the final battle, so he thought that the president was using the new negotiation as cover.

Weeks faulted the State Department for proposing more talks that would do nothing more than extend the war. He knew that he was going to have an interagency battle on his hands, also knowing the diplomats wouldn't give up without a fight. They would continue to stroke the president's ego, playing to his image as a dealmaker. Weeks knew he had to win the fight in Washington among the agencies before he could win the war in Afghanistan.

Cutting the State Department out of the play might make them look superfluous, but he knew he could beat them. Their selling point was to stroke Baron's ego as a great dealmaker, but Weeks realized that was a minor consideration when compared with the image of a triumphant commander in chief. The photo opportunities were too great to be ignored.

———

Stanley Weeks had inherited a staff of people who had loyalties to their former boss. Many of them disliked the way Bolte operated, but they appreciated working for a man whom they considered brilliant. They liked the fact that he challenged them to think of the interests of the United States into the future. Weeks was more lawyerly and seldom confrontational. He told his staff that they worked for the president and they were not to question presidential decisions. He was a team player who wanted the staff to follow his lead. Part of that lead was to pare down the staff until yes-men predominated. Using the president as cover, he wanted to ensure that they followed orders blindly.

After the publicity surrounding his installation, Weeks sought additional presidential guidance. He was given no other directive than to get the troops out of Afghanistan—the quicker, the better. Baron had no ideas and gave the national security adviser carte blanche to do what he wanted. The only cautions were to get the troops out and to make sure that Baron looked good. Weeks wasn't enamored with the lack of guidance because it set him up as a fall guy, but he was a good foot soldier and would do what the president requested.

Calling Dunne and Waddle into his office for a final planning session, Weeks understood they were nearing a decision point. The plan was ready. All that was needed now was Baron's public buy-in.

"Sit down, Abby." Weeks directed his subordinate to a chair at the side of his desk. Waddle stood by the wall. "I spoke with the president a short while ago, and with so many things going on, it looks like ours is the course of action settled upon. He especially likes the idea that if we enter the Zukan Valley, we can destroy the drug trade while closing out the war. He feels it will be a double win for him."

"What about the expansion of the peace talks that he announced?" Waddle didn't like the conflicting narratives. "Are you saying he is going to dump the talks?"

"From my latest reading from him, yes," Weeks answered.

Abby was careful not to burst Weeks's bubble about the president's keenness. "The war plans are good to go, but we have no idea about destroying the drug operation other than to bomb it into oblivion."

"How quickly can you provide me with a full plan with the i's dotted and the t's crossed? The president is in a rush to get this done, so I think he'd approve anything." Weeks was channeling the president's sense of urgency.

"With the work we've already done and with the JCS buy-in, all we have to do is print it and then we're good to go," Waddle spoke from across the room. "We can present a war plan with the hint that the drug operations will be destroyed as a result of it."

"Okay. I'm going to get on the president's schedule so we can give him the full picture." Weeks ended the conversation.

Dunne and Waddle, who made up the NSC planning team, accompanied Weeks to the White House. They had charts and graphs and backup material that they could use to help in answering the president's questions.

Abby Dunne served as the spokesperson. Weeks knew that with her leaning over the Baron, he would not focus on the words but on her. He liked being around beautiful women, and he seemed to follow her every move. When she was done, all that Baron said was "I like it." With those simple words, the plan to expand the fight in Afghanistan was approved.

"I spoke with Erik King last night." The president was referring to the CEO of ISSAC. "He said he could put five thousand contractors on the ground after the military leaves to help prop up the Afghan government. I think that's a great idea, so start putting the pieces in place for that."

The words caught Weeks off guard. The classification surrounding what was planned was so high that officials in government couldn't be told about it, but the president was talking to friends and making plans based on the input of people outside the government. In his time in Washington, Weeks had never seen anything like it.

"You understand that by replacing the military and using contractors, we are going to have to commit more money to Afghanistan. Contractors are expensive." Weeks thought mentioning costs might blunt the president's ardor.

"Don't worry about the money. Using contractors will give me tremendous flexibility. We can use them in any way we want without having to go through the Washington machinery. They can backfill the jobs the military are doing, and the beauty is that no one will give a shit. I'll be free of the worry of having to call some parent to tell them their kid was killed and have the whole nation sob. With contractors, you get the same results—and if one gets killed, that's life. Sure, they make a lot of money, but it frees me from having to pretend I give a shit about some poor kid. Just being free of that burden, as far as I'm concerned, is money well spent." Baron was smug. He didn't like having to be involved in the pageantry surrounding the combat death of a soldier or marine. He thought it to be a waste of his time.

Weeks returned to his office and dismissed the planning team. He wanted some time alone to think about what he was getting into, understanding, when they left the White House, that he owned the plan to end the war and that if anything went wrong, he was going to take the hit. He didn't like the feeling of his vulnerability. It wasn't the way he was used to working, where group decisions were made so that in the event of failure, blame could be dispersed. Now, he had been forced into the position of point man. His was the only name that would be affixed to any failure.

He plopped into his high-back leather chair, feeling defeated, considering what he faced to be a "good news, bad news" situation. The good news was that the president hadn't altered the plan; the bad news, it was looking as if there wasn't going to be a troop withdrawal. It was a troop rotation.

Calling Dunne and Waddle back into his office, Weeks wanted to talk over the things that were bothering him.

"Sit down, guys," he instructed. "I'm comfortable with what we have planned, but we'd better make provisions for a follow-on force of contractors. The president hasn't said formally that that is going to happen, but I'm sure he will decide in the next few days."

"If that's the case," Waddle questioned, "what is the purpose of what we are doing? I thought the entire purpose of the exercise was to reduce the troop strength in Afghanistan. Replacing the military with contractors doesn't make sense under that construct."

"You heard the president. He thinks there is less risk involved when using contractors because while the companies are American, the majority of the lower-level contractors are Third World mercenaries. If any of them get killed, no one will care. I tend to agree with him on that," Weeks added to cut off further discussion.

"Could we reset the problem now that we know what's intended?" Abby Dunne asked.

"I'll listen, but I think it's too late in the game to change anything." Weeks hadn't cut her off.

"If we are worried about casualties, why have ground troops involved at all? We could cut them out and jump right into the air war and obtain the same results."

"That won't fly. The president likes the idea of tricking the Taliban into a ground battle into which he can insert airpower and win the day."

"He does understand that he is risking casualties?"

"It's a minimum risk he is willing to take," Weeks answered, summing up what he thought were the president's aims.

"Explain something to me," Waddle spoke up. "We have been running around covering our planning under a blanket of secrecy. We have people on the staff who have no idea what's afoot, and the president openly discusses this with civilians who have no clearances. What's wrong with that picture?"

"That's the way he operates. We'd better get used to it." Weeks wanted to head off the illegality of what the president had done. "I'm not saying it's right, but the president is the president, so he can change classifications at any time."

"I understand that." Waddle wouldn't be put off. "But now the word is on the street, and I'm sure it will get to the Afghan government. How are were supposed to finesse that?"

"That's a problem for another time. It will be shunted off to the State Department and won't be our problem. We presented the president with a plan that called for ground troops provoking the Taliban to attack. That is still the plan with no changes, so go with it, because it's approved." Weeks could foresee problems and knew that he would own any failure.

In briefing the entire NSC staff, getting the buy-in on what was sold as the president's plan of people who had never gotten their hands dirty in the military was easy. To them everything was abstract, devoid of human suffering. They used big words but essentially looked at the world as a game board for a game in which the United States was always victorious. As a group, they spent less time on planning how to defeat an enemy and more time on plotting how to extinguish the threats they saw coming from other branches of government. They had pretty much given up on accomplishing anything significant in Afghanistan and were hunkered down, waiting for someone to call off the war.

Weeks was aware that he was in for a fight among the staff, but he held a trump card that brushed aside any objections. The president had bought in, making all discussion moot. With that caveat, everyone was compelled to comply or else risk disobeying orders.

Knowing the president might change his mind if one of his friends or business acquaintances were to get to him with a way to make money off the war, Weeks put a top secret label on the mere discussion of the plan. That would control the leaking from his staff and other agencies, but he had no way to control Baron's network of friends and advisers outside the government. For an event that should have had full airing and gone through the rigorous interagency process so that many eyes and voices could develop a coherent plan, there were no challenges from the assembled staff.

As expected, the military resisted. With the peace talks under way to facilitate the United States' extraction from Afghanistan, they couldn't see the need for a battle. They tried to make their thoughts known to the president, but Weeks blocked them. He didn't want to get the president upset, causing him to change everything. Controlling both the process and the information that reached Baron, the national security adviser became a cheerleader for the White House.

The NSC faced more resistance from the State Department because those negotiating with the Taliban had an open channel to the president. Weeks realized that he had to interrupt that channel. He eventually did so by requesting that anything reported to the president come through his office. By inserting himself as a filter into the information flow, he could look at the reports and provide his interpretation. He could cherry-pick the information reaching Baron. He made sure anything the president heard reinforced the idea that he was the leader who was going to put an end to the United States' longest war. The credit for such bold action would be given to the president, and the picture presented was that he could wear a laurel wreath of victory just as Julius Caesar had. The United States could leave the battlefield proudly, saying it had met all its goals in Afghanistan. It could a declare peace with honor, and leave.

CHAPTER 3

THE KNIGHT ERRANT

"Sergeant Major, the colonel wants to see you in his office." A young marine clerk had poked his head into the senior enlisted man's windowless office. It was a dank room lit by bulbs hanging overhead in visible sockets with the wires exposed. There were no reflective shades to augment the light provided; the atmosphere of the room was reminiscent of perpetual dusk. With the US war machine in Afghanistan able to procure anything imaginable, it seemed that procuring bulbs larger than sixty watts was an impossibility. And no matter how many were strung overhead, they didn't put out sufficient light to brighten sandbag walls and corrugated steel ceiling.

The request that the sergeant major meet with the colonel was unexpected. The unit was in the process of packing up and getting ready to depart the war zone. Everyone's mind had transitioned to getting out of Afghanistan. A turnover list had been completed, and all the gear and equipment that was going to be left for the unit replacing them had been inventoried and made ready for turnover. In the final days in-country, everyone's step was lively as all of them thought they might survive and get home in one piece to see their loved ones.

The sergeant major ran over a checklist in his mind. With all the requirements for their departure in place, he could think of no reason why the commanding officer would want to see him.

He walked the short sandbagged passageway to the commander's office, not bothering to knock on the broken wooden pallet that served as the door.

"You wanted to see me, sir?"

"Come on in, Ice." Not referring to him as "sergeant major" wasn't a softening of military protocol. It was a sign of respect for the enlisted man. The colonel and he had a history. Almost twenty year earlier, several miles from where they now sat, they had served their first tour of duty in Afghanistan together. The then second lieutenant Dan Keefe and lance corporal Jaio Santiago were bloodied in the same firefight. Keefe had never led a platoon in combat and was struggling, trying to direct his undermanned platoon through a remote village in search of a suspected terrorist cell. It was a mission that called for more personnel, but Keefe's platoon was operating with only two squads, missing a third of its firepower. Twenty-seven marines were in enemy territory with a vague mission. A nervous vibration ran through them. The young marines respected Keefe because he had their best interests at heart, but with this being his first foray into war, they questioned themselves internally, hoping he knew what he was doing. Doing things by the book, as new officers did, was good, but they wondered how he might react when the bullets started to fly.

Santiago was in the squad, bringing up the rear, and could see all that was taking place ahead. The marines were descending a hill, approaching a village consisting of a dozen sun-dried brick huts. The homes sat at the bottom of a bowl along a muddy, slow-moving stream that provided irrigation water for root crops. It was hard to tell what the people were growing because the wind that swirled over the village, which was surrounded by hills, trapped the air in a circular flow and picked up the thin layers of topsoil, depositing it on everything, making the scene a monotone of tan silt. Even the crops took on the color of the sand-impregnated air, which made the green leaves dirty and drab. The scene laid out before the marines was meager subsistence farming. No one could believe there was enough food produced to feed the inhabitants.

Squads had difficulty finding cover as they moved downhill, following a treeless footpath. Their exposure caused the hair on the backs of their necks to rise, much like animals when they are presented with threats. Being in the last squad, Santiago wasn't as worried about approaching the huts as he was of the hills on either side of their approach that restricted the unit's ability to maneuver. Mounds of brown dirt resembling sand dunes narrowed into a slot that was less than fifty yards wide with little protective covering. For the whole time it was going to take the marines to escape their vulnerable position, they were going to have to do so exposed.

Since the lead squad was concentrating on the village, Jaio started looking at the hills around the notch they would have to get through. He couldn't see any enemy, but he kept thinking it was the perfect place from which to conduct an ambush.

The first shots were fired from the village. The marines hit the dirt, trying to burrow in, making themselves one with the ground. The lucky ones found rocks to hide behind. Keefe, wanting to move the lead squad to one side of the notch while bringing up the drag unit, was running forward to position the marines, when he was hit and went down, away from cover.

He lay in the open. Every marine knew instinctively that he was being allowed to lie there writhing in pain as a lure for others to try to save him. The platoon sergeant, the only marine who had combat experience, set the marines up to engage the hostiles in the huts, then made a quick dash toward the lieutenant. He was steps away when he was taken down in a hail of gunfire. The young marines were essentially leaderless now. No one was willing to take on the responsibility of making decisions that might get others killed.

Santiago didn't get emotionally invested in what was happening. He assessed the situation. The lieutenant and the platoon sergeant had to be rescued, but no one had a plan amid the confusion. Taking the mantle of leadership from marines who outranked him, he did so calmly.

"The shots that downed Sergeant Kirby," he said calmly as if the situation was normal, "didn't come from the huts. They came from the crest of the hills to the north." He pointed to high ground ahead of them. "It looks like the people up there stay hidden until shots are fired from or at the huts. The firing must signal to them that they should expose themselves to engage a target." Santiago was one of the youngest marines but was in control of his emotions, causing the others to listen to him. "The lieutenant is bait, but we don't know how long they intend to let him live, so we have to get him and Kirby back under cover." He didn't ask for volunteers. "I'll go out and drag them in, but here's how we're going to do it." He made the marines part of the solution. "First squad, I want you to focus all your firepower on the huts. When this thing starts, I want to be sure the people there will keep their heads down and not worry about killing me. Second squad, cover the hills. I don't think the people up there will show themselves until they hear firing, but when they do, they should make decent targets because they have to get to the forward face of the hill to have firing angles. Regardless, I want enough firepower on them to make them crawl back." He waited to see if marines outranking him had understood what he had said. Seeming to get their concurrence, he explained what he was going to do: "I'm going to move myself as close as I can to the lieutenant and Kirby. Don't waste ammo until I take my first steps in the open. Got it?" The young marines could believe one of their own had taken control of the situation. More impressive was Santiago's calm. He was going to risk his life and seemed unconcerned.

Santiago moved to a position closest to the wounded and peeled off his body armor, all his heavy gear, and his helmet, laying it all on the ground.

"What the hell are you doing?" he was asked by a corporal who outranked him. "Our orders are to wear protective gear at all times. When the command finds out about this, you're going to be in trouble."

"Corporal, in case you haven't noticed, we are in trouble. If we survive this, I'll take the hit for peeling off my gear. Besides, the extra weight will slow me down, and I'm going to have to be quick." Raising his arm, he lowered it quickly and dashed to the wounded. The firing from the huts started immediately as he exposed himself. The Afghans, knowing what he was intending, concentrated their small arms fire. The firing was intense before the marines in the first squad could start their suppressive fire. It was a bit late. Jaio felt a searing pain in his face, as if a hot knife had slashed him. The pain didn't stop him. As he continued, he could hear the second squad firing at the hills to the north. With all targets engaged, he believed he had a window of opportunity to get Keefe and Kirby back to the protection of the unit. He didn't have time to position them, just grabbed them by their gear harnesses and dragged them like sacks of potatoes to the marines.

Santiago's actions and his control of his emotions earned him an honorific from his peers. He became Ice. He was no longer referred to by his rank or his nickname, Chill, a moniker that had evolved during his time in the corps when a drill instructor, thinking it showed some sophistication to know the capitol of Chile, referred to Santiago as Chile. None of the recruits had picked up on the drill sergeant's attempt at derision. They assumed the drill sergeant was referring to the food that they were served often in boot camp. That label stuck until Santiago left Parris Island. When he joined his first unit, the marines, not knowing the evolution of the nickname, shortened Chile to Chill.

In the chaos of bullets flying overhead, where minds became a scramble between panic and survival and reactions were confused in an effort to live another minute, things slowed down for Santiago. He was able to think beyond the chaos. He moved as if he had a plan, thinking one step ahead of what he was facing. Frightened marines of his age and rank marveled at his demeanor. Wrapping bandages diagonally across his face to cover his wound, he'd had to cover one eye, but he could see the marines in the platoon didn't want to move from the protective cover that they had found. He wasn't angry. He called the radio operator over, asking for the call signs of the units that were in support. Contacting the battalion air officer, he calmly requested a medevac helicopter and a fire-suppression mission to drive the enemy off the hill. None of the marines in the platoon knew how he had learned to communicate with the airplanes, but he directed them to their targets. When the area was safe, the medevac was called in and Keefe and Kirby were loaded onto it. The marines around Santiago expected him to get aboard with his wound, but he waved the helicopter off with just two wounded. Santiago, knowing the marines were leaderless, felt a responsibility for them. He led them by having the most senior marine give the orders that he had instructed be carried out.

The wound Santiago had suffered healed, but it left him marked for life. Where the bullet had slashed across his face, it opened a half-inch channel that knitted back together, leaving a scar running the length of his right cheek. As the skin healed, it tightened, pulling up excess flesh, which caused Santiago's lip to curl slightly, leaving him with a perpetual sneer. It kept people at a distance, which was too bad because Jaio was a warm person.

As a sign of respect, the marines he had served with in combat dressed up the nickname Chill to Ice, then to Iceman, which is that name stuck up and down the chain of command. Iceman wasn't always the most senior marine on-site, but his reputation loomed over those around him.

Santiago had been decorated for bravery after a fight over the award he should receive. Dan Keefe, his commander, put him in for a Navy Cross. Everyone expected the award to be issued. However, the awards board in Washington had issued only a few Navy Crosses to officers, and it was thought that an enlisted man shouldn't receive the country's second-highest award for bravery when so few officers had. They admitted that what he had done warranted the medal, but they said it wouldn't look good for an enlisted man, especially a lance corporal, to be walking around with a Navy Cross. So, Santiago's award was downgraded to a Silver Star. He knew of the fight surrounding his receiving of the award had created, and he accepted the Silver Star with the same cool dispassion he had displayed in battle.

Jaio Santiago had grown up in the decaying section of Fall River, Massachusetts, a city that had seen its textile mills flee, leaving hollowed-out buildings and people. The destruction left behind was a graphic display of capitalism at its finest. In a search for cheaper labor, the booming mill economy was shuttered overnight and moved south, where the labor was inexpensive. Unemployed people hunkered down as they watched their standards of living plummet. They scraped by any way they could, but it was always a fight to survive. Sons and daughters were born into poverty with little hope of escaping. They could ease their fall only with booze and drugs. Jaio's grandfather had been a drunk, and his father had gone a step farther and died of a drug overdose. That was the future available to Jaio unless he somehow broke the pattern.

Unlike his friends who accepted their fates, he had a plan. He was going to stay clean and escape the life presented to him. While his father had been alive, his life was chaotic with family disruptions always centered on picking his dad up off the streets and hoping rehab would work. It didn't. When the old man died, Jaio's mother became the primary breadwinner. No matter how hard she worked, she could never get ahead. Therefore, a trail of evictions and utility stoppages followed the family. In the depravity, Jaio noticed something courageous about his mother: no matter how dire the family's circumstances, she always put her kids' well-being first, and somehow there was always food on the table. For a woman who had little formal education, she pushed her kids to study so that they could get good jobs and wouldn't have to undergo the humiliation of lifelong poverty.

Jaio was the only son in a Portuguese family. Because of this, his mother doted on him at the expense of his sisters, but they didn't resent the attention he received. There was something about their brother that was unlike any of the kids in their circles. He was smart and reserved, offering his opinions occasionally, but when he did so, those opinions were usually correct. With the family living in the projects, home to the poor of all nationalities, Jaio learned to communicate with people in their respective languages. He was fluent in both English and Portuguese. The housing projects where he lived abutted a French community, and in order to procure certain items and get things done, he had to learn French. By the time he had reached ninth grade, he was conversant in four languages. He had an ear that could pick up tonal nuances—and he liked the idea that he could communicate. It helped him to better understand others. When a Syrian family moved into the projects, he became friendly with their children and worked to talk to them in their language. He wasn't as fluid in picking up Arabic as he was the romance languages, but he tried.

It was apparent that Jaio was going to grow larger than anyone in the family. The family lore had it that a great-grandfather had been a giant of a man, but in the succession, no one had grown over six feet. Jaio hit that mark when he was fifteen and was sought after by his high school coaches who watched him in physical education classes and marveled at his athleticism. No one could understand that a person with his size and, as it turned out, his natural speed would turn down the glory that could be attained on the sports field, but Jaio passed up athletics for a job in a clam shack doing all the dirty jobs associated with cooking and serving deep-fried foods. He used his meager pay to ease his mother's burden.

Working menial jobs opened his eyes to the life that was about to swallow him. He started thinking about those things that would allow him to escape. All his life, he had been told how good looking he was. Working around girls and women who wanted to get married, he found it easy to have quick sex in any number of places, even behind food fryers. He was seen as a catch, and he enjoyed the bodies offered, but he realized it was all a one-way road to nowhere. Girls and women who offered themselves wanted to continue on as they were. Jaio understood that if he didn't plan for himself, he was going to be stuck with a wife and kids.

Trying to distance himself from the temptations, he turned inward. Such behavior made him seem aloof, and that made him more alluring. In looking for a way out of his preordained life, he became an avid reader. He didn't limit himself to one form of media. If he wasn't with a book, he was at the high school using their newly arrived computers to research something that interested him. It was in the school library that he got an invaluable education. The librarian, a middle-aged woman, became interested in the good-looking young man who showed so much interest in books. When she discussed what he was reading, his demeanor changed; his dour expression faded and he smiled, exposing perfect white teeth. With everything about him hinting at his Portuguese heritage, the smile seemed to change his persona. It stood out against his olive complexion, which was unmarked. His hair was tight knit and black, the front running down almost to his black bushy eyebrows, so when he opened his eyes wide, he almost lost his forehead in the hair. He had a broad nose that contrasted with a narrowing chin that had a deep dimple. He was a boy who could get by on his looks, but his large brown eyes seemed to gather information, and when he spoke, his voice was deep and resonant. He was a man-child; both girls his age and women much older wanted to marry him.

An assistant football coach who was trying to date the librarian wanted to get Jaio out of the library. He wasn't sure, but he thought with all the time Jaio spent with the librarian, they might be having sex. Knowing he could use a player of Jaio's size and athleticism, the assistant coach devised a plan that was going to satisfy both his wishes. He sent three of the larger players to intimidate Jaio into getting out of the library and joining the football team. The trio cornered him in a six-foot space between the brick school building and an exterior stairway. A confrontation was unavoidable. With the players puffing themselves up, readying to fight for the school's honor, Jaio didn't listen to their threats. He calmly looked them over, gauging their weaknesses. Only one of the boys, the school's star linebacker, was aggressive, but Jaio saw, in looking into the eyes of the school's two tackles sent to back up the linebacker, that they didn't want to be there. They stood behind the linebacker and kept looking backward over their shoulders for an escape route. They weren't emotionally invested. It was the linebacker who was looking for a fight to make the coach proud. Jaio let the others fade from his mind as he focused on the threat. In boyish exuberance, the linebacker, out to force his intentions, with both hands shoved Jaio backward. Jaio had foreseen the assault and had braced himself. Instead of moving backward away from his attacker, he moved to the side, where the two boys who were supposed to provide bulk stood. The move surprised the attacker, but not as much as Jaio's fist, aiming for his nose. The sound of the impact made it known to all that the nose was damaged. The two boys who'd been sent as muscle took off, and the schoolyard, which moments before had been full of kids, emptied as if a claxon had sounded. The fight was over. The linebacker was on the ground hurt, and Jaio was the only one around to help. Jaio took him to the school nurse, who confirmed that the nose was in fact broken. The nurse did what she could but had to call for an ambulance to transport the boy to a hospital emergency room. For the entire time she was working, stemming the flow of blood, she watched Jaio. She had seen the results of dozens of schoolyard fights, and all she ever saw was the beaten student as everyone involved in the fight disappeared. The injured were dumped off at her door as students vanished to avoid any responsibility. But Jaio stayed in her office, obviously concerned. When the ambulance arrived, she couldn't believe Jaio went to the boy he had hurt and encouraged him that he was going to be all right. The nurse couldn't believe that a sixteen-year-old was willing to take the responsibility for his actions.

Jaio had won a Pyrrhic victory, winning the battle and losing the war. The assistant football coach, incensed that his plan had failed and that his star was out for the season, wanted Jaio out of school, where other students might look at him as someone who had defied the coach. He testified that he had observed the fight from a distance and that it had been instigated by Jaio. With false testimony, he pushed the principal to have Jaio expelled.

Without school as a sanctuary, Jaio could see his life spiraling downward. For a while he worked full time and helped out the family, but he felt trapped. He had to rise above others' expectations of him, but every time he applied for a job that would allow him to think about a life outside the projects, he was told he couldn't be hired without a high school diploma.

"Mr. McGrady, I need to work more hours. Do you think you could schedule me for more?" Jaio asked his boss, the owner of Mac's Clam Shack.

McGrady was a Vietnam veteran with one crippled arm as a result of the war. He wasn't a surrogate father to Jaio, but he had taken an interest in him. Over the years, he had hired hundreds of high school students and had never seen one with Jaio's intelligence or drive.

"What the fuck is wrong with you?" McGrady wasn't scolding him. "Why do you want to work more at a shitty job like this? Look at you. You stand behind a bank of fryers cooking greasy seafood that isn't that good, but people keep coming back for it. You smell of cooking grease, and you go home tired every night. You're better than this. Jaio, I know you are supporting your family, but if you don't escape this town and the Clam Shack, you're going to be doing shitty little jobs for the rest of your life. Do something to break out of this town. Join the army. Do something." McGrady, realizing that he was preaching, changed his tone. "Okay, if you need more hours, you can work as much as you want."

What McGrady had said had been on Jaio's mind, but he didn't know how to break out of the downward trace of his life. "I tried to join the army. They wouldn't take me without a high school diploma."

"We'll get a GED. They'd take you with that."

"What's a GED?"

"I don't know the right name. All I know is that if you take a test and pass it, it's the same as a diploma. Get one and no one can turn you down for a job that requires a diploma."

Jaio showed no emotion, but it was if a light had just gone off in his head. He sensed that he had found an avenue of escape.

Jaio had heard of a GED but had never thought it would play in his life. He now sought the help of the high school librarian. Things had changed since his expulsion. There had been charges brought against her for abusing a minor and the school was going to dump her, but when they came to Jaio for his testimony, he would not turn over on her. In his sworn statement, he verified that at no time had she touched him. With that, she could not be fired. He had lied, but so what. He knew what he was doing and was aware that there were other trysts going on among the faculty at the school. He was a willing party and saw no reason for her to suffer. Since he no longer was seeing her—that was too dangerous for both of them—he did ask her advice about the general equivalency diploma.

She found that he was age eligible and met all the requirements for taking the GED test. She thought that he could pass two areas of the test, reasoning through language and social studies, because he had spent so much of his free time reading and these were the subjects that when he was in high school he'd always aced. She was wary of the math and science parts of the tests, but she managed to get some practice tests. She couldn't tutor him, so he had to go through them on his own.

It was going to cost him sixty dollars to take a pretest, but the librarian told him she thought he could pass the real test, so why waste the money?

Jaio had his GED before the class he should have graduated with had their diplomas. He couldn't celebrate with the librarian. The only person he felt he could talk to who would understand how he felt was McGrady.

As Jaio walked into the Clam Shack for his shift, the old man could see a different person.

"So, you got your diploma. Now, I suppose, you're going to quit and leave a hole in my schedule."

Jaio hadn't thought about that and didn't want to let McGrady down.

"This ain't about me. This is about you. You've got your diploma, so use it as a ticket to put Fall River and this place in the rearview mirror. I've hired a lot of high school kids in my time here, and you're different. You've got smarts, so use them to make a life for yourself." Mc Grady wanted Jaio to know that he didn't owe him anything.

Leaving work that night, Jaio was torn. For the first time in his life he had a choice, a life-altering choice, to make. He was struggling with what to do, when he was informed that his sister was pregnant and that she and her boyfriend were moving into his mother's small unit in the projects. Life would be impossible. It was like a light switch had been flipped. Jaio decided he would leave his family and get away.

Showing up at work early, he wanted McGrady's advice. McGrady was one of the few adults whom Jaio trusted.

"Great," the older man said enthusiastically, "you decided to get out of here. That's good. My advice is not to look for a job around here. You might make good money, but you're still here. Put some distance between you and anything associated with Fall River. That way you won't feel tempted to come back." He stopped. "The easiest way to escape this shithole is by joining the military. I hate to say that, because this is my souvenir from my time in the military." He extended his withered arm toward Jaio. "This is what I got for getting away." He paused and looked the boy over. "There are ways to get around something like this. Join the air force or the navy. They don't get their hands dirty, and they get to march in all the parades with the guys who hung it out." There was a tinge of bitterness in McGrady's voice, but he quickly became more positive. "The advantage of the air force and the navy is that they have jobs that require skills that you can use when you get out. They'd send you to school to become a jet mechanic or a computer guy, skills that you can sell when you're a civilian. Christ, if you were a jet mechanic, you could get a job anywhere but in Fall River. There isn't much use for jet mechanics around here. Whatever you do, stay away from the grunts, because shit like this can happen to you." He held up the arm again to emphasize his point.

Jaio spent most of the day thinking about his future. Standing over a hot fryer cooking clams, wishing he were somewhere else, he couldn't concentrate on his work. He thought about the career options that he and McGrady had talked about. Being a computer tech didn't excite him. He couldn't see himself working indoors for the rest of his life. The more he played with his options, the more the idea of being a jet mechanic captured his imagination.

All the armed services recruiters were located in the white marble and colonnaded post office with offices adjoining. Jaio had made up his mind about the air force. That was the branch of the service that would offer him the best career opportunities. He arrived at their offices to get information about what career options they could offer him.

He was greeted by a sign saying the office staff would be back in one hour. He was disappointed. He had chosen the air force over the navy because he didn't like the idea of spending time at sea. His few attempts at working on fishing boats hadn't worked out well. He was sick most of the time he was on the water, and that translated into what he thought navy life would be like. With an hour to kill before the air force personnel returned, he took a seat on a bench outside their offices.

"Can I help you?" asked a marine recruiter who had walked past him.

"No. I'm just waiting for the air force office to reopen."

"That may be awhile. They're making a presentation at a high school down on the Cape. If they run long, they probably won't be returning today." The marine placed doubt in Jaio's mind about the viability of waiting. "Are there any general questions about the military I can answer for you?"

"No."

"I take it from the fact that you're here looking into the air force that you're also looking for a skill that will help you when you get out of the service." The recruiter knew how to sell.

"That's what I came for. I wanted to see what it would take to get trained as a jet mechanic."

"That's a great skill to get. When you get out, you could turn that into big bucks." The recruiter dangled the bait. "I'll bet you didn't know that the marine corps flies the most sophisticated jet aircraft of any of the services. I've put a couple of dozen people into the jet mechanic pipeline, and I've got vacancies now. I could give you some tests. If you passed them, I could guarantee you a slot in one of our jet mechanic schools. In fact, right now, I've got a need to fill some seats. If you pass the tests, I can get you shipped out within two weeks." The marine, having set the hook, awaited Jaio's response.

"When could I take the tests?"

The recruiter knew he had him. "Tell you what. You show up here Friday, and I'll have all the testing material ready for you. You can take the test, and when you pass it, we'll sign you up."

Jaio passed the test, but a hurdle remained. He was too young to join the military and needed his mother's approval, but she didn't like the idea of having her son leave. She wanted her family around her. To Jaio's surprise, she refused to sign the required waiver.

"Do you have the papers you need signed?" McGrady asked after listening to Jaio's problems.

"Yes." Jaio took the papers from a folder.

"What's your mother's name?"

"Alma."

Placing the papers on a flat surface, McGrady took out a pen and signed Alma Santiago with a flourish so that the name was hardly distinguishable. "There. Now you're good to go."

"Is that legal?"

"Of course not, but no one is going to know that your mother didn't sign unless you tell them, so keep your mouth shut." McGrady smiled. "That's the second time I've done that. My parents wouldn't sign when I wanted to join the marine corps, so I signed for them. That turned out to be a bad idea." He held up his withered arm and paused for an overly long time. "This also got me some of the best friends a person could have. A couple of them were killed, but, man, were they good kids. One of them gave his life to save me, so I didn't have the right to bitch when all I got was a useless arm."

Jaio saw a side of McGrady he had never seen. The crotchety businessman was replaced for a moment by a man who had a past that he was proud of. Although scarred, he reveled in what he had done.

"You won't have to worry about getting shot up. Stay in the jet mechanic pipeline and you'll come out okay."

When they talked for a while about marine corps boot camp, Jaio had the opportunity to see a man he hadn't ever really known. McGrady's memories of his experiences were both warm and humorous. He spoke freely to the boy as if he were admitting him into a club.

Jaio, along with a busload of boys and young men, stumbled off the bus and were herded to the yellow footprints painted on the tarmac at Parris Island, South Carolina. The whole procedure was confused. Sergeants in tight-fitting pressed uniforms yelled instructions and scolded those who made wayward movements.

The day was a blur. Things seemed to settle only when the recruits in their ill-fitting uniforms found themselves standing in front of their bunks waiting for their drill sergeant to introduce himself.

Sergeant Dowd walked down the aisle between the recruits standing on either side, looking disdainfully at the human garbage he was expected to, and would, mold into marines. Dowd was a marine who could have been model of military perfection. His uniform was contoured to his six-pack abs, and the short sleeves of his shirt could barely contain the muscles of his weight lifter arms.

He started down the line of recruits on Jaio's side of the building, berating and scolding each one individually. His sharp tongue had the recruits wondering if they had made a mistake joining the marine corps.

It was Jaio's turn.

"What kind of a name is Santiago?"

"Portuguese."

"What are you, some kind of Mexican trying to pass yourself off?"

"No, sir."

"Didn't you hear me tell these other vermin that I ain't a sir? You call me sergeant."

"No, Sergeant."

"Speak up. I want everyone to hear you so I don't have to repeat myself."

"No, Sergeant."

Usually when Dowd went through his act to get more volume, the recruits showed nervousness, but he detected no such nervousness coming from Jaio. The boy standing before him was several inches taller and raw boned.

"I told you to speak up."

"No, Sergeant." The words almost blew Dowd over, but he detected no fear, so he decided this was the recruit he was going to break.

"Since you can't speak up, get down on the deck and give me twenty push-ups."

Jaio did twenty push-ups but didn't stop there.

"I told you I wanted twenty. Are you willfully disobeying my orders? Get on your feet!" the sergeant screamed. "Are you stupid? Can't you count? How many did I tell you to do?"

"Twenty, Sergeant."

"And how many did you do?"

"Forty-one, Sergeant."

The number triggered a reaction in Dowd that the recruits weren't expecting. He backed away from Jaio, confused. A bulletin had been issued that no recruit was to be given more than forty push-ups in one day. Dowd wondered how Jaio knew of that number and if he himself was now in trouble for letting him reach forty-one. He looked at Jaio warily and moved on. He was going to have to determine if the recruit had set him up for discipline.

The attacks in New York and Washington occurred during the last weeks of training, at which time the atmosphere at Parris Island changed. Every recruit knew that promises of specialty training would not be honored. The entire recruit class would become grunts.

After graduation, when newly minted marines were cleaning and packing their gear, the assistant drill sergeant informed Jaio that Dowd wanted to see him.

Knocking on the door as he had been taught, Jaio was told to enter. It was the first time he had ever seen Dowd relaxed.

"Sit down, Private Santiago."

Jaio did so warily.

"The reason I called you in is because I know you're disappointed about not becoming a jet mechanic. You did everything right while you were here and were the honor man of the entire company. You should have been sent off to the air wing, but for the marine corps' sake, I'm glad you weren't. We're probably going to get into a shooting war, and the corps is going to need leaders. You've got something that none of the other recruits I've dealt with have. I can't explain leadership and what it takes to be a leader, but you've got something that makes people want to follow you. After four weeks, I could have turned the platoon over to you and you could have done the job I was doing. So, I've concluded that your value to the marine corps is in leading troops, not turning wrenches. That said, it has been a pleasure training you. I hope that if and when a war starts, we can serve together."

Dowd stood and came around his desk to shake Jaio's hand.

⁓

"The colonel wanted to see me?" The sergeant major knew the answer but posed the question anyway.

"Yeah, Ice. Come on in. I have something I have to run by you." Keefe sat behind a gunmetal-gray desk that was buried under papers. His red hair was graying at the temples, and there were tufts missing from his head where he was balding. He was on his last tour and had submitted his retirement papers. Now he was just playing out the string until he could return home and become a civilian again. "I just received an order telling me to stand down getting the battalion ready for departure. Apparently, there is a special mission coming our way. The whats, whys, and hows weren't given to me. All I was told is that we are to stand down because a mission is coming."

"That doesn't sound good. Most of our gear is staged for our rotation."

"I know." Keefe paused and thought about his next words. "This is going to be a bitter pill for the troops to swallow, but those are our orders. I was thinking we might head off a mutiny by gathering the battalion and breaking the word to them, as much as we know. It will piss the marines off, but I think giving them the bad news up front is the best way to do it. It will put us out ahead of the rumor mill that is sure to start up once messages start flying."

"The marines are thinking about nothing but getting out of here. A change so close to departure is going to seem like a jinx and will get them to worrying about getting killed." The sergeant major paused and took stock of the problems that would face the marines in the battalion. A change so close to escaping the war zone uninjured was sure to dampen morale. Young marines would do what they were told, but they would do so with the weight of knowing they were on the line when they shouldn't be, which would cause a lot of grumbling.

"Where did the orders originate?" The sergeant major was trying to determine the reasoning behind the change in plans.

"I received a call from a marine friend in the Pentagon telling me this was coming our way. He had no information other than that the military has been locked out of the planning for this, what appears to be a special mission. He wasn't sure, but he thinks the planning originated in the NSC or maybe even the White House." Keefe stopped. He was at the limit of his knowledge and had no more he could share. "I've called up and down the chain of command in-country, and no one has heard a thing. I think I might have stirred a hornet's nest because I've received a flurry of calls asking me what I know. No one up the chain has any idea of what I was talking about."

Santiago mused, "This has the earmarks of a plan that might vanish in the light of day, when people up the chain get their chops in it. I'd hold off on gathering the troops and getting them riled until we have something concrete that we can give them."

Keefe accepted the senior enlisted man's suggestion. "I'm going to work the phones for the rest of the morning. How about we get together at noon and I'll give you any updates that I receive." He dismissed the sergeant major.

What started as a trickle of information from a Pentagon friend soon became a flood. Keefe had two phones working. As much information as he received, he was left to cut through the hearsay and rumors. Everyone he spoke to had a theory, but no one could tell him things he needed to know. By the time his noon meeting with Santiago arrived, he had nothing substantive to share.

"I've learned a lot this morning, but most of it is garbage. No one can nail anything down. It's like there's a mission for us floating in the air. A lot of people know of it but don't know anything about it."

"I might have had better luck," Santiago commiserated. "I spoke to the top enlisted man at the presidential squadron that flies all the VIPs around the world. He said a C-17 has been ordered up for a flight to Kandahar. He couldn't tell me who would be on board, but he did say that the request came from the White House. He's sure it won't be any of the big players because no additional security was requested. He checked around and found out that the passengers will include some White House staffers and several people from the NSC, but he had no names. With that information, I called a retired marine who is a glorified gofer at the NSC. He told me the plans for this mission are originating there, but he also said the entire NSC staff has been cut out of the planning. A small group is coordinating everything, and nothing is leaking. He did say that the planning, whatever it is, has been done in conjunction with the White House. He guesses that the president's hands are all over this."

"That can't be good," Keefe mentioned.

Santiago smiled in agreement. "Apparently, the personnel involved are going to leave Washington tonight. With the time changes, they are scheduled land about midmorning the day after tomorrow. Helos have been laid on to get them from Kandahar to here. I guess by midafternoon a day from now we will have the puzzle solved. The other tidbit of information I gathered was that the information we are going to receive is so sensitive that only a face-to-face briefing will do. There will be no paper trail. The people arriving want to keep whatever they are going to tell us secret."

"What a way to run a war," Keefe spit out in disgust.

"You know, Colonel, this brief we're supposed to get hasn't been vetted through the military. It's like people who planned this war haven't yet realized that this isn't a game of Risk where you push flags around a game board and capture whole countries based on some off-the-wall strategy. In the little wars we get to fight, where people face off to die for a patch of dirt, it ain't so easy."

"Well, if your information is correct, we'll have what the best minds in Washington can tell us as to why this battalion is wrapped up in their schemes. In the meantime, let's keep it cool and, as best we can, stamp out the rumor mill, because once the arrival of the C-17 is announced and helicopters are scheduled to fly the people here, things could get crazy."

The sergeant major had been in the marine corps long enough to know that pop-up missions had a way of going off the rails. His fear was that the people from Washington would get marines committed to something that was going to get them killed. The briefers would be back in their offices in Washington, sipping their coffee, while marines would be bleeding in Afghanistan. He hated being cynical, but what he had heard thus far had a stench to it.

The only requests the battalion received prior to the arrival of the party from Washington was that they have a secure conference room ready. The group of briefers didn't want to spend too much time in an area where people might get killed. The marines were told that they would be departing once the brief was completed. That seemed odd. Visitors from Washington usually liked to mingle with the troops and have dozens of selfies taken so that they could show the people back home that they had experienced war. The other strange request was that the number of personnel to attend the brief would be limited to the commanding officer and his senior staff. The reasoning was that the classification of the brief was so high that only the personnel indicated could receive an on-the-spot classification that would allow them to listen to what was being said.

Keefe and the sergeant major stood well off the windblown landing pad, awaiting their visitors. As the helicopter landed, it raised a dust cloud, obliterating sight. The greeting party had been dusted over enough to know how far away to stand.

Three men and a woman who was dressed like a man stepped off the helicopter and stood in the subsiding dust. They wore suits and ties under their flak jackets that made them look like stuffed sausages. They wore head protection and goggles and had expected a more elaborate reception than that which awaited them. Not knowing what to do, they milled around as the helicopter shut down.

When all was quiet and the dust was gone, Keefe and the sergeant major moved forward to greet their guests.

"Welcome to hard times," Keefe joked.

The guests didn't know how to take the comment. They hadn't expected such a bare-bones encampment. The marines' camp had been gouged out of the highest point in a desolate landscape. They could look down on everything, but there was little to see except rolling sand hills with scrub trees that were thwarted in their growth by lack of water and the constant wind that bent them over. The people from Washington hadn't known what to expect, but they could never have imagined the harsh conditions that faced them. They were aliens in a world not to their liking, regretting that they hadn't ordered the marines to fly to Kandahar, where the facilities were better.

"I'm Colonel Keefe. This is Sergeant Major Santiago." The marines expected some response, but it was apparent that the guests weren't there for pleasantries.

"Do you have a secure briefing room set up?" the apparent leader asked without introducing himself.

Keefe had greeted dozens of visitors, some important, some not. He didn't like the attitude these Washingtonians displayed.

"It would help if we knew who you are. Unless we do, I can't let you into the secure briefing facility."

Recognizing the marine's anger, the leader decided to introduce his team. "I'm Barry Waddle, and this is Abby Dunne from the NSC. This is Jim Elder and Howard Bates from the White House." Keefe wasn't listening to the names. He was interested in their titles. Each held an important position and was willing to flaunt it in a land where titles meant nothing.

"Would you like a chance to freshen up before you start your brief?" the sergeant major asked. It was common for visitors after the long flight from Washington and the dusty helicopter ride to be given an opportunity to go to the bathroom.

"No, we'd like to get started," Dunne answered for the group.

The sergeant major had seen many visitors process through the battalion but had never seen a group as tight-assed as these people.

Keefe led the visitors to the awaiting Hummers. He hopped into the lead vehicle with Santiago.

"This ought to be fun." He was referring to the coolness between the Americans from Washington and the Americans on the ground in Afghanistan. He couldn't imagine what their briefing would entail.

"I guess in the hour they are going to spend here, they'll tell us everything we are doing wrong and solve the war puzzle for us."

"I think you're right." Keefe laughed. "Let's give them the benefit of the doubt. Maybe they have some new stats that will show us a new way of doing things."

The Hummers entered the built-up marine encampment, which was a series of blast walls and thousands and thousands of sandbags piled so that they covered the sides of the many hastily built structures. Dust and the sand colored anything standing above ground level.

Keefe led the visitors to the battalion conference room, but it wasn't what the visitors expected. The furniture was covered with sandy grit.

The visitors moved to seats behind hastily made paper nameplates. Each was reluctant to sit in the dirty folding chair provided or to place their elbows on the sandy table.

"Sorry about the accommodations," Keefe apologized, enjoying the discomfort of his guests. "But this is a basic setup for all marines in-country. The surroundings aren't fancy, but they work for us. I hope you don't mind." He looked over the seated guests. "I believe we have everything you requested, so I'll introduce my staff." He had directed his comment at the White House staffers who seemed rude, giving the impression that they were superior to the marines.

The introductions didn't soften the tensions.

"Let's get started." Abby Dunne took over. "We instructed you that we wanted only senior staff who had security clearances that we could update to the classification required to receive this highly secret briefing." Looking specifically at Keefe, she said, "You're going to have to dismiss your sergeant major."

The colonel, surprised, was angered at the request. "Ma'am, I don't really give a shit about the bogus clearance level you've put on this brief. In fact, I don't care if only you and the president are written into the classification. If my staff is cleared, the sergeant major is cleared. If you can't buy into that, you can pack all your paperwork away and head on home."

"You don't understand, Colonel. This is a briefing for a high-priority mission."

"And since you're here, I suppose that marines of this battalion are going to be involved in it. If there are going to be my marines involved, the sergeant major stays." Keefe laid down a marker.

"What do you think, Barry?" she asked Waddle, the anointed classification officer.

"We can raise the sergeant major's classification before we start briefing," Waddle reluctantly conceded.

"Can we begin?" Dunne asked, as if she had been whipped.

"We're all ears." Keefe gave his okay.

"First off, gentlemen, I want to stress the importance of the secrecy surrounding what we are going to brief and what the marines will attempt. At no time will reporters be briefed on what is occurring, unless the approval comes directly from the NSC staff. We don't even want imbeds sniffing out this story. To ensure that doesn't happen, all press credentials will be revoked and all the press people currently working with the battalion will be recalled. If all works as planned, they are receiving their notices of recall as I speak and will be on the chopper out of here with us. That said, reporters will be fed into the battalion as the NSC deems necessary. Is that understood?"

Since it was what was going to be ordered, the marines nodded their understanding.

"Can someone start the overhead projector?" Dunne asked.

The marines smiled to themselves. The people who had been sent to them to brief them on a secret plan were helpless in the face of having to plug the projector into the socket provided.

Keefe looked at the sergeant major and rolled his eyes.

With a white wall illuminated, Dunne placed her first graphic on the projector. To no one's surprise, it was a map of Afghanistan, on which she pointed to the location of the marines and their proximity to the Zukan Valley. She displayed nothing that the marines hadn't already seen and fought over, as there had been fighting in that location for nearly twenty years. She went on to explain the economic importance of the valley to the Taliban drug trade. When she was assured she had laid the proper groundwork, she placed a slide on the projector that told the audience that the remainder of the brief was top secret and could be discussed only with persons who had a need to know. When she was sure that the gravity of what she was going to brief had sunk in, she displayed overhead photography of the Zukan Valley and began discussing the planned mission. Taking a positive tone, she talked about the simplicity of the plan and the fact that no additional military assets would be required, adding that the mission could be run at any time. She downplayed the part the marines would play and stressed that aviation would essentially win the battle. She spoke for a half hour before concluding and asking for questions.

Several of the battalion staff officers asked questions, seeking to understand their roles in what was briefed, but Dunne had no answers and deferred to Waddle for most of the questions. Waddle was equally at a loss for answers. He was a big picture kind of guy who had no concept of the sacrifice the troops would have to make for his plan to work.

"Does anyone else have questions?" Keefe had heard enough and wanted to get the Washingtonians on their way. As he spoke, he looked toward the sergeant major, whose jaw was so tight in anger that it looked as if his face was going to break. "Sergeant Major, do you have something to add?"

"Yes, sir." He took a deep breath, realizing that he was the firewall, lending some sense to the decision to send marines to the Zukan. "With all due respect, ma'am, sirs, that is the dumbest fucking thing I have seen in the seven tours I have done in this country. What you're doing is baiting a mousetrap with marines— and you are going to get them killed."

"The president has approved of this plan," Jim Elder from the White House staff shot back, thinking the implication of the weight of the office would silence dissent.

"What your beef, Sergeant Major?" Keefe wanted to hear everything Santiago had to say.

"Apparently, no one involved in planning this has read history. If they had, this plan would not have gotten this far."

"Everything I've briefed has been approved at the highest levels." Dunne was willing to fight for a plan that she herself had played a large part in developing.

"Who is going to take the responsibility when it all falls apart and we start sending bodies home?" Santiago threw out a counternarrative.

The question stunned the group from Washington. In all their planning, there had been no mention of failure. The initial thought of it had them squirming in their seats.

Dunne relented. She was no longer the insightful Washington whiz kid, and she didn't want the taint of failure associated with her name. "Could you explain your objections, Sergeant Major?" It was the first time she had recognized the enlisted man as a person.

"The Zukan Valley is almost a duplicate of the valley at Dien Bien Phu." Santiago threw out a name that he thought might register, but he received only blank stares. "At Dien Bien Phu, the French were going to try to do what you are suggesting for the Zukan. They were going to stage a set-piece battle that was going to draw the Viet Minh into a fight that would win the war and thereby allow the French to extricate themselves from a war they were tired of. They placed battalions of their best paratroopers on the ground, hardened troops who had been fighting in wars for years. They thought with an overwhelming force and with airpower, they were going to draw the enemy in and rout them. They didn't expect that half-starved men and women would be able to carry artillery through the mountains. The Viet Minh knew of the French's counterbattery capabilities and the fact that they had airpower, so they dug their artillery into the back sides of the mountains ringing the valley to negate those advantages the French had. When the fight started, the Viet Minh had already registered their artillery on landing strips, negating resupply other than by paradrop. When the weather turned bad, airpower proved useless. As you probably know, their plans for a glorious victory failed."

"Times have changed. We have the most sophisticated aircraft and air delivery systems." Waddle jumped to the defense of his plan. "We have at our disposal aircraft that can attack day or night, in good weather and bad. Our airpower can defeat any ground force, ensuring that we could win the battle."

The sergeant major stood his ground. "We've been bombing the cave complexes ringing the Zukan Valley for nearly twenty years with sophisticated and experimental weaponry, and we haven't been able to destroy them. On every patrol I have been involved with, we found little damage after our aerial attacks. What we did find was that each cave had an established firing ring." He looked at the blank stares of the guests. "That is a prep site that must be established before a mortar baseplate can be laid down. What will happen is that the Taliban will carry their mortars to the sites and set them up in three minutes or less. And they will be preregistered." Again, the sergeant major got blank stares. "Ordinarily, when a mortar is being set up, there is a leveling process that takes time. And then it takes time to register mortars on targets. The firing rings allow all that to be accomplished in minutes. Several mortar rounds can be fired that will hit predesignated targets. Then the entire operation can be broken down and the mortars pulled back into caves, where aerial bombing will not damage them."

"The plan is not to attack enemy forces other than those that engage the marines. The intent is to destroy the entire valley," Waddle chimed in.

"Are you saying you are going to bomb civilians?" Santiago didn't like the sound of wanton killing.

"What we are saying is that it is our intent to destroy anything in the valley tied to the drug operation. That may entail collateral damage, but it will allow us to claim victory." Elder had just provided the actual reason for entering the valley.

"To what end?" Keefe asked, not liking what he was hearing.

"It will give the president cover in pulling our forces out of Afghanistan." Elder hadn't answered sheepishly. He was in on the planning and was proud of what was being proposed.

"What happens when all the carnage of the aerial bombardments is over and I have a company of my marines trapped in the valley with perhaps two thousand Taliban fighters eager to kill them? What is the plan to extricate them?" Keefe was angry, which could be seen in the redness of his face.

"Air cover will prevent the Taliban from making a strong attack against the marines."

"What the hell is 'a strong attack' supposed to mean? It sounds as if you are willing to write off marines as part of a PR victory." Keefe was relentless.

"This operation has been analyzed and run through computer models. If any marine lives are lost, they will be minimal, well within the acceptability quotient." Elder looked toward his group for backup, but they knew he was selling a product the marines in the room weren't buying.

"Mr. Elder," the sergeant major interjected, "it appears you have sold the president on a flawed plan. Marines, along with Afghan civilians, are going to die. How large a body count is it going to take for this to be called off? Because there will be bodies on both sides. If this is Washington's way of selling out the Afghans, why not use the Kurdish model and say that the Afghans didn't help us at Normandy and then pull out? After all, isn't that what the peace talks were about, giving us an exit strategy while leaving the carnage that will take place after we leave to others?"

"Sergeant Major, your commander in chief is ordering this mission. He knows that in war there will be casualties, but he deems them acceptable in the larger picture of establishing a lasting peace." Elder thought that by invoking the commander in chief among the marines, they would fall in line behind the plan. He failed to realize that some in the room could possibly be quantified as collateral damage. A man with no skin in the game was telling people who might die that their opinions didn't count.

"For this to work," the sergeant major added, "it's going to take a much larger force on the ground, because when the last bombs have been dropped, those marines on the ground are going to have to fight their way out—because the Taliban will still control the cave complexes ringing the valley. By using less than a company, you're writing a death sentence for those on the ground. Is there a possibility that the number of troops could be raised to give us a fighting chance?"

"I understand your concerns, but the plan I presented was the one the president signed off on. He won't back away from it." Dunne let the words sink in. The marines had their marching orders. It was their job to comply. With the marines around the table seeming subdued, she wanted to finish and get out of hostile territory. "There will not be a normal chain of command for this mission. The in-country chain of command will be bypassed. This will all be run out of the NSC. It is being done that way so that you will get everything you need. It is felt that by doing it this way, the airpower that will be essential for this mission will not be siphoned off. All you have to do is request it and it will be there."

"That sounds great, but we lose contact with Washington randomly several times a day. What happens to our air support if we can't speak to Washington?" Keefe was trying to blow a hole in the way the command structure was set up.

"That hasn't been mentioned before, but I'll cover that when I get back to Washington." Dunne paused, searching for an answer. "We'll set aside airplanes that can be utilized using the in-country chain of command. If we should ever be out of contact, you will be able to call the planes as you normally do." She was satisfied with the answer.

"Why not avoid any glitches and let us use the normal chain?" Keefe asked. He saw what was being proposed as an ad hoc plan that had major flaws.

"It has been set up this way so that the president can play in the decision-making. There is a war room for him to move things around in what he considers to be the best way to fight the battle. With that said, all the press relations for Angel Fire"—Elder used the code name for the operation—"will be controlled from Washington. There will be no reporters with the troops on the ground. Everything is classified, so that means none of the marines involved will carry personal smartphones. We want no texts or selfies of this operation released. This operation will be run in the dark, and only when it's over will the marines involved be able to speak about it publicly. If you look at what will be attempted, you'll see this is a cut-and-dried operation. A company, or less than a company, of marines will enter the Zukan. They will be met with resistance, and the air war will commence. It will pound these people who are just out of the Stone Age back into it and will give the president a victory that he can use in ending the United States' longest war.

"Are there any questions?"

No marines raised their hands. The Washingtonians took it as a sign that they had sold the president's war plan. The marines sat dumbfounded, in disgust.

It was impossible to keep a secret in the marines' camp. Once Company A was signaled out, rumors flew. Some hit on the exact mission, while others ran the gamut of craziness. Regardless of where on the spectrum of correctness the rumors landed, none of them did anything to raise morale. For a unit that was packing up to go home to be told they were being held in place and would be part of what was considered an important mission had soured their dispositions. Santiago didn't like the change in mood. The marines in A Company, a unit that was the battalion's best, were disinterested in getting their gear reissued so that they could get back into the fight. The negativism bothered him. Instead of thinking about how they were going to stay alive and survive their tour, the marines felt they had been screwed, and cared about nothing that lay ahead. They were only concerned that they missed the boat home.

Santiago brought those concerns to the commanding officer. "Do you have time to talk, sir?" he asked as he poked his head into the CO's office.

"Sure." As Santiago entered the sandbag-walled room, Keefe asked, "What's on your mind?"

"I don't like the way this mission is shaping up." The sergeant major paused.

"Are you going to tell me what's on your mind, or am I going to have to guess?" Keefe joked, knowing the senior enlisted man would pull no punches.

"I'm not going to get into the specifics of Angel Fire. You know that I think it's fucked up and that it is going to get marines killed. I'm worried about what I'm seeing in A Company. The attention to detail that they need when getting ready to go into battle is missing. The marines, looking at what they have lost, feel jinxed. They did their duty and got through their tour, and those who survived feel this mission is going to get many of them killed. The unit cohesion that is needed when going into the fight is missing, and every marine is looking at friends and keeping them at arm's length, not wanting to get too close to someone who might die after they had nearly succeeded in getting out of Afghanistan."

Keefe cut him off. "I see the same things, and you and I have seen enough of this war to know these kinds of head games are usually disastrous. What's worse is that we don't have the power to change what's coming our way."

"But we can give A Company a better shot at surviving this."

"How?"

"Captain Dorn," Santiago said, referring to the A Company commander, "was rotated out a week early for medical reasons. We've been using Lieutenant Walsh as acting company commander. That works when all we are doing is packing boxes to return to the States, but this is something altogether different. The lieutenant is completing his first tour and has only been bloodied in a firefight once. He doesn't have the experience needed to lead this clusterfuck."

"As you and I discussed, switching one of the other company commanders over to lead the company is rife with pitfalls. There isn't enough time for them to learn the strengths and weaknesses of the marines they'll be leading. They couldn't learn enough about the marines in that time to know whom they could lean on and who couldn't do the job."

"Yes, sir, I agree, but throwing Lieutenant Walsh into the fire, which will probably become a major conflagration, isn't going to do him any good, nor is it going to do shit for the marines."

"Ice." Using the nickname, Keefe broke down the barriers of rank so that they could talk freely. "I've known you long enough to know you've got something on your mind. Talk to me."

"I don't want to badmouth the mission, but it's a made-for-TV event. When it's over, the actors, dead on the battlefield, will not get up and dust themselves off for another action scene. It's using marines, not in the national interest, but for a PR splash."

Keefe stopped him. "You're not telling me what's on your mind."

"We don't have a company commander, and the platoon commander whom we've moved up doesn't have the experience to lead something like this. That's not good. What I'm going to suggest may sound weird, but it covers a lot of bases."

"We've done weird," Keefe joked, thinking that nothing the sergeant major could tell him would be shocking.

"Maybe not this weird." Santiago didn't crack a smile.

"Well, knock me off my feet."

"I'm the only one in this battalion who knows the troops and has the experience to pull this off. I'm thinking the mission will have to be subverted if the marines are going to have a chance to survive. If it is subverted, you can't put that responsibility on the shoulders of a lieutenant. It would ruin his career and, more importantly, might get him killed."

"Jesus, Ice. Are you telling me you want to lead this?"

"Yes, sir."

"That is weird. An enlisted man leading a company in combat. I don't know if that's possible."

"It is. First of all, this isn't going to be a full-strength company. It's going to be two platoons plus a few support troops. You won't

73

have to replace the platoon commanders; just take them off the troop list so that we can move platoon sergeants into command positions."

"That won't fly with the planners in Washington. They want officers whom the president can talk to so that he can be seen as delivering orders to his officer corps. That will make him seem like a real general." Keefe spoke to the realities of the situation.

"Colonel, I know I don't have to tell you this, but this isn't going to be a play war. My gut feeling is that the marines are going to be the losers. Not the marine corps, but a bunch of nineteen- and twenty-year-old kids. If the president ends up talking to an enlisted commander, sell it as a PR coup, the idea being that he really cares for the troops."

"I can see that you are dead serious, and I know you're not just gunning for medals. You have enough of them already. You're leaving out a piece of this. I really need to know what you're thinking before I set in motion something that will get us all fired." Keefe was nearing the point where he was going to have to decide, and he wanted all the facts.

The sergeant major paused. "The mission is flawed, and the only way marines are going to get out alive is by selectively implementing the orders received. Some are going to have to be ignored, and some will have to be disobeyed. The marines are going to have to go into survival mode immediately. I know what has to be done in the Zukan, but it would be better if I kept you in the dark. That way, when the shit starts flowing our way, you will have plausible deniability."

"Are you sure you know what you're asking me to do?"

"Yes, sir."

"If I approve, what are you going to need me to do?"

Santiago thought over what he was going to request. "I'm going to need Gunny Wells to serve as my number two, and then I'll need two staff sergeants from Charlie Company, Washington and Coburn, to serve as platoon commanders. They are all the best in the battalion with the experience needed to run troops."

"That can be done, but since you're playing games, I'm going to have to play a little too. You can have the people you want, but in the initial troop lists I send to Washington, I'm going to have to include officers' names. They can all get the green flu just before you kick this off."

"Colonel, I feel bad for getting you involved in this. It may turn stinky."

"They pay me the big bucks to make career-ending decisions." Keefe laughed. "I can't wait to see what the planners in Washington are going to say when they see the final troop list. The shit will hit the fan."

The three enlisted men who were to serve in officers' positions were called to the sergeant major's office, where he laid out what he thought might happen. Santiago specifically wanted to inform the men he had chosen that they wouldn't be doing things by the book. Every event and encounter was going to be accomplished with the purpose of keeping marines alive.

"I picked you guys out of all the NCOs in the battalion because of your reputations for being the best, but more importantly, you were chosen because the troops look up to you. You staff sergeants have been platoon sergeants and have worked with platoon commanders long enough to know how a platoon is run. And, Gunny, you'll serve as my executive officer, doing all the coordination to keep this whole thing together. This as a suicide mission, and rules are going to be made up as we go along. Some of the shit we'll have to do may scare you, but the endgame in all instances is to keep marines alive. There are going to be twists to this mission none of us has experienced. Once we get into the field, the battalion will cut us loose. Orders will be coming to us from Washington, maybe even from the president."

"That won't be too fucked up," one of the staff sergeants joked.

"Now you're beginning to understand that this is no ordinary cruise we'll be on." Santiago smiled along with the others. "That said, you're going to have to utilize all the tricks you've learned in your tours here to stay alive—and maybe play games none of us has ever played."

"Sounds easy." Gunny Wells shook his head in disgust.

"I know the information that I've passed out isn't much, but this mission, from top to bottom, seems as if it was conceived on a cocktail napkin. There hasn't been any thought given to the marines other than they are going to be bait, and like all bait, marines can be wasted to catch a fish. The emphasis is on the air war. Airpower is supposed to win the war from thirty thousand feet. The good news, so I've been informed, is that we will have access to multiple air platforms, and if our radios work, we should be able to talk to them and call them in on targets. Staff Coburn, since you have had forward observer training, you are going to be our man coordinating between ground and air. Now, since you haven't worked with the troops you'll be leading, go out and meet them. Your reputations will be enough for you to be accepted." Santiago paused. "I know you'll have questions, but hold them off until I learn a bit more about what we're supposed to do, besides being sitting ducks."

"I don't want to steal the sergeant major's thunder, but there are a couple of things for us to think about," Gunny Wells chimed in before they broke up. "From what the sergeant major has told us, this is going to be a made-for-video war game. Airpower is going to win the battle no matter what we do on the ground. We're bait, and it would be a good idea for all of us to think about the fact that no officers will be along with us. That makes us cheap bait, easily expendable, because no one is going to give a shit if a bunch of enlisted grunts get wasted. As you think about what you are going to have to do, think about that."

Santiago was glad he had chosen Wells as his number two. Wells had a cynic's view of the war, and that had kept him alive.

While the sergeant major kept Keefe out of his planning, he had to use the assets that the battalion could call into play. Therefore, he requested that a civil affairs team be sent to the Zukan ahead of troops being deployed there. He specifically requested that the civil affairs personnel barter with the magistrate of Naaz, a small town on the Amu Darya River ringed with mountains. His guidance to the team was that they were to negotiate for a plot of land that was different from that which the planners from Washington had selected. Unlike the piece of ground picked for them, which was in a natural bowl and close against the mountains, the parcel Santiago wanted was away from population and amid a landscape that was rutted where mountain runoff had gouged wadis into the ground. The land wasn't arable, was well outside the agricultural and poppy-growing zone, and was pitted and rocky with depressions where the marines could find cover from the mortars that Santiago knew ringed the valley. The fact that it was remote and was terrain that no military would select for setting up a base camp gave him hope that the enemy had taken these factors into account and hadn't bothered to preregister their mortars there. The upward-sloping land was the ideal location from which to prevent overland approaches by an enemy ground force. And he thought that with the rock outcroppings and some clever marine digging, he could make the area less vulnerable to overhead fire.

Keefe was on board with the use of the civil affairs team, but he questioned going to a magistrate of a town rather than the provincial governor.

"Why the magistrate?" He was curious.

"They're both crooks, but the magistrate runs the Taliban."

"The intelligence doesn't indicate that." Keefe wasn't arguing. He was stating what he knew.

"There is an inverted power structure in the province. In reality, the magistrate runs the governor."

"I know you've studied this part of the world and have put in the time to learn the language, but we spend a lot of money on intelligence to know what's going on here. And our best guess is that the governor, although a crook, is in charge."

"Colonel, during the initial US incursion into Afghanistan, when we were trying to oust the Russians, the mujahideen faction we worked with was led by Hekter Aziz. We weren't sure of his politics, but Aziz was willing to do our dirty work for money. After the Russian rout, our people, the CIA, wanted to install him as governor, but he refused under the guise of wanting to get back to the land to live a simple life. We bought into that narrative, hoping he was a patriot, and continued to use him. By my calculations, he has been on the CIA payroll for nearly forty years and is considered a prime intelligence asset. If you look at him, you see he lives like royalty, making no pretense of living in poverty, which is the Taliban tradition. Such a deviation from Taliban orthodoxy should get him killed, but he is left untouched. No one knows how rich he is, but he controls the drug trade in the Zukan Valley, and of course continues to be paid by the CIA. Our intelligence people have looked at him and have written him in as a drug dealer who pays the Taliban to stay in business. My sensing, after having been in Afghanistan for this, my seventh tour, is that nothing moves in the valley without his buy-in. When he was working for our intelligence people at the very beginning of the war, he was working out of Pakistan because he has strong family affiliations on both sides of the border. He could live in either country with ease, but the CIA, in trying to use him as an asset, set him up in Afghanistan to compete with clans they had no control over. He has been given a pass by our people and the Taliban. The Taliban pass is important because he's allowed to stay in business and prosper."

"Is that your sensing of what's happening in the province?"

"Yes. And while I hate to contradict our intelligence experts who place all their focus on different individuals, I must say that the magistrate is the man."

"Is that why you want the civil affairs team to set up a meeting with him?"

"Yes, sir."

"Should I ask what you are planning to talk about?"

"Sir, remember when we first discussed this and I told you that I wanted to afford you plausible deniability? This falls under that construct. I may be bending a few rules, but everything I do will be with the intent of giving the marines who are stuck with this mission a chance to make it home. I'm not evading your question, but I intend to sit with the magistrate and discuss survival, his and ours."

"Ice," Keefe said, bringing the conversation back to the familiar, "I have complete confidence in you, but I have finally seen why you requested to lead this mission. You are going to do things that no officer would attempt. I sure hope it works."

"I think by doing it my way, the marines will have a better chance to survive. If I'm wrong, things won't be any worse than what has been handed to us. We are bait that Washington wants to use to start an air war. They are willing to take marine casualties to spring their trap. It is the move of every desperate nation when trying to end wars. It serves no purpose in Afghanistan. The world knows we are leaving and, in so doing, leaving the Afghans high and dry. Somehow, a pseudobattle is supposed to give us cover to pull out honorably. It won't cost much, just a few dozen marine lives. I'm not willing to buy into that. Our marines deserve better."

―――――

The marines set up their camps in Zukan Valley, bypassing the site the Washington planners had picked for them. Abby Dunne reported the breach in the plan to her boss Stanley Weeks, and they sought answers. They had wanted the marines positioned on a flat, open stretch of ground where they were sure to be attacked. In the location Santiago had selected, the marines were a harder target, and that might delay taking enough casualties to start the air war. It was the marines' vulnerability that was going to make for a quick start to war.

79

Since the NSC had cut out the normal channels of communication, they were forced to talk to Keefe, who denied issuing the order for the change. He didn't know why the marines were not at their assigned location but would find out and report back, he'd told them. The story he'd reported was that the magistrate of Naaz, Hekter Aziz, refused to cede the ground to the marines. The only place he would let the marines encamp was on a scrubby piece of land rolling from the foothills north of the valley. It was a cover story that didn't sit well. The NSC had no idea who Aziz was, and they didn't care, other than he had introduced a delay into their plans. The two people charged with the plan's execution, Dunne and Waddle, had overlooked that there might be local opposition before the fight began, but they pretended that they had foreseen both the problem and the location given to the marines.

At their new home, the marines immediately became mole people, trying to dig their way underground. Santiago assumed that they would have a few days' grace period before the Taliban decided how they were going to eject them, so he had them dig and dig deep. No perimeter surrounded the camp. It was hoped the interlocking small arms fire would serve as an impenetrable wall.

Leaving the grunt work to the gunny, Santiago was going to meet Aziz to determine if there was some way to hold off the Taliban. He assumed if anyone could do it, it would be Aziz. In his research of the magistrate/warlord, he determined that Aziz was considered a tough negotiator, a man who always wanted something in return for anything given up—and the sergeant major had little he could offer.

"Sergeant Major, you can't drive into town alone without security. Let me put a team together so that you will not be killed," the gunny complained as Santiago climbed into an open soft-top Hummer that had the canvas laid flat, like the back of a convertible. Everything in the vehicle was exposed, including the sergeant major.

"It'll be all right," he consoled, not sure of his own words. "Aziz knows I'm coming, so I figure I'll have free passage this one time."

"Sergeant Major, everyone knows your reputation, but what you're going to do is batshit crazy. If you drive into town unarmed, you'll be the only son of a bitch who isn't packing. You've got to carry a weapon."

Santiago was amused at his subordinate's concern. He was in fact concerned, but he wanted to meet with Aziz as no other American had met the magistrate. He intended to arrive at the meeting without a weapon or body armor in an effort to show the local kingpin that he didn't fear death. That was important to an enemy head who was willing to sacrifice himself for an ideal. Santiago knew, on his drive into town, that the audacity of what he was doing would precede his arrival and would cause his host to wonder what the hell he was dealing with.

"Can I go along with you to ride shotgun?"

"Gunny, you're needed here. If I go down, you're going to have your hands full.

"I feel useless. Is there anything I can say that will make you make this trip in a more up-gunned way? You know, with body armor and guards, and maybe a Hummer with a fifty-caliber mounted, kind of as a show of force."

"There is something you can do. I saw one of the troops carrying a boom box. I didn't know they made them anymore." Santiago smiled upon conceding that he was out of touch with the real world. "Go find him and see if I can borrow it."

When the overly large music player arrived, Santiago didn't know what he was going to hear, but he turned up the volume and listened to some noise that sounded as if it had a beat.

"Tell whoever it is who owns this that if it gets destroyed, I'll make it good."

"The marine isn't worried about the box itself, but he said he loaded it with five of his best discs and wants to make sure he gets them back. He said they would load automatically, so you should have about an hour and a half of music. Since we have instructions on not destroying his music, how about thinking about not getting yourself destroyed?" the gunny said gloomily.

"I'll be okay." With those final words, Santiago drove toward the town, listening to music he had randomly heard and which he was sure the Afghans had never heard. Passing the first group of walkers along the road, he waved to them. The natives seldom looked up when US vehicles passed, but upon seeing a lone marine listening to weird noises, their curiosity was piqued. They followed the American with their eyes, wondering what the hell they had just seen.

The casual drive continued down a main street of a town that looked as if it had been platted to be perfectly square. It was crowded with foot traffic and animal traffic, and every person seen was armed. Santiago's presence in their midst confused them. They had no instructions on how to act, so they let the American pass, assuming that Aziz had approved his being there.

The man Santiago was going to meet was an American by-product of the war. As a young man, he had fought and had distinguished himself as a mujahideen fighter, catching the eye of the CIA. They were looking for fighters who would go against the Russians and destabilize their war efforts. In an area controlled by the Ganzi tribe, Aziz was an outlier. He was a fighter with no tribal structure to back him. The Ganzi wanted him out of the valley, and while he was fighting for the Americans, they continually tried to undermine him. Without tribal protection, he relied on the CIA, who had issued a hands-off decree that let him continue. Understanding where his power was coming from, Aziz started using the CIA to weed out his enemies. In the viable intelligence he fed to the CIA, he inserted the names of any tribal leaders who opposed him and thereby let the CIA eradicate them.

With the dispatch of the Russians, US assistance to Aziz was abruptly stopped and the Ganzi were ascendant once again. The tribe that saw its path to power through governance took over many of the key positions in the newly formed government, including oversight and use of the Afghan army. Aziz felt threatened and, needing help to fight off the Ganzi, aligned himself with the Taliban, a group of young fighters much like the mujahideen who fought to make Afghanistan an Islamic state. Aziz didn't believe what the Taliban preached, but he needed their ability to provide him with fighters in trying to hold off his enemies.

After 9/11, the CIA had shown up in Afghanistan in force and sought to reestablish ties with the man who had worked so well for them. In their absence, Aziz had learned how the US system worked. Money moved everything in the war. He signed on with the CIA and no longer received payments covering a time span; he was paid for piecework. Everything he did had a price associated with it. It was money the Americans willingly paid. They were looking for results, and Aziz provided them with such. His was the only force that would go into the mountains and look for al-Qaeda. With his successes, the CIA lionized him as their man.

As US money poured in, Aziz was able to fund his own army. He settled in the Zukan Valley, where the best efforts of the Ganzi to oust him were repelled by the CIA. When they needed a mission run that the military couldn't handle, the CIA went to Aziz, paying him well regardless of the outcome. He was their success story, the man who was providing the best HUMINT, and they paved the way for the expansion of his businesses.

The Zukan was an historic opium poppy–growing valley that had lost its significance between the wars, but with the world market demanding more supply, Aziz saw an opportunity. He took his troops and made them soldiers/farmers. In two years he had established a growing and distribution system that was throwing off money to pay to the Taliban.

Several times during the war, efforts were made to shut down the Zukan opium monopoly by the DEA and other agencies wanting to cut off the money flowing to the Taliban, but those agencies didn't have the CIA's clout. They came to Aziz's defense because he was still providing them with intelligence and doing some of the dirty work they wanted done.

Understanding that the US efforts in Afghanistan were about spending money, Aziz started a construction company. He had the Americans pay for road networks in and out of the Zukan. The cover story was that good roads would attract visitors to cultural sites, but the roads allowed for the freer flow of drugs. The Americans didn't care. The Aziz construction company made money, and the American consultants and contractors employed there made even more money. It was a game with little accountability. The only thing required was that at the end of the project, the Americans could take pictures and convince themselves that they had done a good thing for the Afghan people. Money showered down like the spring rains, but unlike the rains it nurtured nothing, until Aziz sold the CIA on the idea that an irrigation system should be developed for the valley. The cover story was that with a good irrigation system, the Afghans might be able to shut off the opium growth and turn their efforts to vegetable farming. The Americans, having fallen in love with the idea, poured money into irrigation ditches and pump houses to get the Afghans away from growing opium poppies. Everyone on the US side was ecstatic. The euphoria lasted for one growing season, until it was found that with irrigation, the poppy crop was quadrupled. Aziz owned the water rights for the valley and had amassed power by being able to control the flow to the Taliban in an effort to keep them in his camp, all thanks to the Americans' naïve intentions and ill-thought-out plans.

The biggest scam, and one that Aziz couldn't break into, was the training of the Afghan army. Billions were being spent, and there were no reliable units. Every year a new US firm came in, promising to train the Afghans, but the results were the same. Soldiers could march in straight lines but couldn't be counted on in battle. Aziz wanted part of those contracts but had been shut out. He was baffled. He could take a cadre of young men and train them into a fighting force in two weeks, whereas with billions spent and years involved, the Americans got nothing. Aziz then realized the training was unimportant. What was important was the money American trainers made.

Santiago thought he had a good picture of the man he was going to meet. He expected him to have a guerilla's tough mentality, looking out for his own interests and looking to make a buck as the Americans had taught him.

It wasn't hard to find the Aziz building complex. The buildings were the only ones standing higher than one story and the only ones that were constructed of materials other than adobe bricks. Another indication of the complex's importance was the number of armed men lingering about. A small army was employed to be sure Aziz remained safe. It was a necessary precaution. There was too much money involved with the drug trade. Competitors continually came forward to try to take Aziz's share.

As the sergeant major stepped out of the Hummer, he left the boom box blasting. He didn't know how long the music CDs would last, but he wanted to give the guards something to think about. His instinct was correct. As he moved away from the vehicle, the armed men closed in and looked at the device that was creating the strange racket. None of them dared touch the sinful device, but they looked at it as if it might transform itself into the devil.

Santiago walked to the building, toward a door that he guessed protected Aziz. Any guards not transfixed by the boom box eyed him. They had never seen an American without body armor or a helmet, and most wore goggles or some kind of eye protection, so the Afghans never got to see their eyes. Instead of the caricature of an automaton, they saw that Santiago, although a little taller, was as slender as they were. Without a helmet, his black hair was like theirs, and his olive skin, while not as weather-beaten, reminded them that there might be similarities. They didn't see an enemy soldier. They saw a man who could bleed and die as they could. Because of this, they wondered what he was doing in their midst. As most of the men huddling around bore the scars of war, they were transfixed by the scar that ran across Santiago's cheek, realizing that if the bullet that created the scar had moved one inch either way, it would have killed him. Men who had, for their entire lives, dodged bullets understood what it meant to be lucky on the field of battle. The marine's scar served as a badge of honor among them. They allowed the American to pass with grudging admiration.

A guard stopped Santiago at the entrance and frisked him, patting Santiago down several times, looking for a weapon. He couldn't believe he didn't find one. Unsatisfied with his failure, he had the sergeant major remove his shoes, which the first guard inspected as another guard rubbed Santiago's feet to be sure he was not carrying a bomb. Indicating that the marine could put his shoes back on, the guards spoke among themselves. Not understanding that Santiago could speak their language, they ridiculed him as being crazy, but in their slander was a hint of respect.

Once Santiago was allowed to enter the building, he saw that the office in which he stood could have been the front office of a US business. Desks were lined in rows. The difference was that there were no electronic devices on them. In place of computers and phones were boxes stuffed with papers and men hunched over them in what Santiago assumed was some effort at record keeping. Even criminal enterprises had to know where the money was.

Santiago was led through the phalanx of desks. Then his escort knocked on a large wooden door at the end of the room. It opened a crack. When those outside had identified themselves, the door swung open and the marine was allowed in.

The room had the appearance of a doctor's waiting room. Chairs neatly ringed the walls, surrounding a colorful Afghan rug, but there were no tables with out-of-date magazines. People who got this close to Aziz were there on business and didn't need entertainment.

"Sergeant Major," a young man speaking slurred English greeted the marine. "I'm Mr. Aziz's interpreter. I'm surprised you didn't bring your own interpreter."

"We couldn't find a Pashto speaker, so I'll have to use you to interpret."

The young man was astounded. The marine wasn't bothered that he might twist the interpretation. "Magistrate Aziz will see you as soon as he finishes with the people he is doing business with. Would you like a seat?" He pointed to the chairs.

Whoever it was with Aziz didn't come out through the waiting room. A buzzer sounded, and the interpreter said, "We can go in now." The inner office didn't pretend to be that of a business executive. It dripped of opulence, its crowning feature being a full-length painting of Aziz in his tribal garments. It was impossible to ignore, as were dozens of paintings of him in regal poses. A man with such an ego wouldn't have brass trays and goblets sitting on tables. Santiago assumed that he was being offered a drink in a gold cup.

Aziz was a head shorter than the marine, but even in his business suit he looked hard—the kind of hardness one develops after years of fighting to survive. His eyes were penetrating and were as richly dark brown as those of the marine. He said something to the interpreter that Santiago understood. "Who is this fool who has come to see me unarmed? The Americans must be getting desperate."

"The magistrate greets you," the interpreter said to Santiago, easing the comment.

"Tell him that it is my honor to meet such a great man and noble warrior." Santiago wanted to hear what the interpreter would say. If he could understand him, he could dispense with him.

"He said he comes unarmed because the Americans couldn't afford ammunition." Both the magistrate and the interpreter laughed.

Aziz spoke to the interpreter, then the interpreter said to Santiago, "The magistrate would like to know how you would like to start. He has no idea why you are here."

"I'd like to speak to the magistrate alone," Santiago said in slow but understandable Pashto. As he spoke, he watched Aziz. The startled reaction was seen in his eyes, along with a knowing that he had to be wary of the man across from him.

"Take a seat." Aziz pointed to a plush leather chair along the wall and took a different seat so that he could look directly at Santiago. "You can leave." He waved off the interpreter.

"You are a wily enemy. You come into my camp understanding many things. I'm sure you know that I have the power to wipe out my enemies." Aziz laid down his marker. If he wanted, he could have the marine killed. While wary of the sergeant major, he was fascinated. Aziz had worked with the CIA and the Americans for nearly forty years, and he had not known one who had respect enough to learn his language. He considered the Americans colonists, so he used them and took their money under the guise that he was their man.

"I'm not here as an enemy. I come to seek your help."

"Americans are never my enemies." He pointed to plaques on the wall issued by the CIA, commending him for his service.

"You have to consider the marines who have arrived in the Zukan as your enemies."

Aziz stroked his black beard. While it was bushy, a blood scar ran through it, starting at his chin and sweeping upward over his left eye until it was lost in his hairline. It was his warrior's scar, which gave him status among the people. They knew that in any fight they entered, he would be there leading them. He assumed from Santiago's scar that the marine, like him, wouldn't run from a fight.

"You are here because you are in a bad situation. Your marines were sent here to die as sacrificial goats to inflame American passions and allow your country to commence an air war unlike any seen in Afghanistan. Your blood will be the lubricant that loosens the gears of a destructive war."

"What you say is all true, but you have something to lose." Santiago didn't know how Aziz could have known about the air war. He had learned of it only days before in what was supposed to be a classified briefing.

"Yes." Aziz thought about what Santiago had said. "Did you know that eleven marines will have to die before your air war starts? Will you be among them?" He paused. "You may well be. You see, you have already angered those who conceived this idea. They wanted your camp set up on the flatland. That was sure to get to the number eleven quickly. When you placed your camp in an inaccessible location, you threw off the timing of the war. It may take longer to get to the required number of killed. That has angered many of your people. They are also angered that you, a sergeant major, are in command of the marines. Their plan was to send junior officers who would obey any order no matter how insane. With you, who have experienced war, they feel you may not follow their dictates precisely. As a result of your placing your camp in a location that they didn't select, you confirmed their fears about your questioning orders."

"You mention eleven marines dying. Where did you get that figure? I have heard nothing of numbers." Santiago was curious.

"You forget that I work with the CIA and other American contractors. They said eleven will be the trip wire to commence the air war. It is not too few and not too many. The number was decided upon by whoever conceived of this war. My informants also indicated that all your missions will come out of Washington and your combat operations will be followed by an assigned drone to ensure you comply with the orders you receive."

Santiago knew there was a kernel of truth to what Aziz said. He had already heard rumors of the Washington planners being angry with him, but Keefe had so far managed to hold them off from doing anything to remove him. He wondered about the drone and, if true, how Aziz could have known about it. Aziz seemed to know more about the US planning than the marines.

"I know about your plans because the contractors, before they rushed to leave the valley, gave me a hint of what was afoot. For nearly twenty years, there has not been a day where an American contractor hasn't been draped on me, trying to get something out of me. When they rushed to leave the area, I knew the air war that they described was coming was going to kill indiscriminately." Aziz looked at the marine with an intense glare. "You and I are the ones with the power to ensure hundreds aren't killed for no reason other than for that which could be gained at the negotiation table."

Santiago was stunned. He'd just been told by the Afghan that he had powers that he was unaware of.

"I have a proposition that will benefit both of us." Aziz was blunt. "The size of the marine force in so vast an area is meant to bait a trap. You have the weapons to beat back Taliban attacks for a while, but that is not the point. A Taliban attack will be a trigger mechanism. There are many things an assault could trigger, and none of them are good for the marines or the people in this valley. Your dying will unleash all the air assets in Afghanistan." Aziz turned a notepad with names and figures on it toward Santiago. "You can see the airplanes that will be used and the bases they will be flown from. Buildings, roads, irrigation networks, and bridges essential to the drug trade will be destroyed and businesses will be flattened. The brick plant, which has nothing to do with drugs, will be destroyed—for no reason other than to prove you are capable killers."

Santiago knew that brickmaking was part of Aziz's legitimacy, his cover story.

"There are only two dozen structures in the valley that are more than one level. That doesn't make for good movies. The brick plant is big and tall, so I'm sure it will be destroyed several times just for the movie footage." Santiago was cynical.

"My American handlers have not mentioned this to me." It was said as if Aziz should have been informed by people he knew, not a marine who spoke his language. "The CIA wouldn't let this happen. We have an arrangement."

"Have you heard of the Kurds?" Santiago asked.

"Yes, of course."

"They had arrangements, and that didn't work too well for them. You are in the same position. The president wants to leave Afghanistan in much the same way he wanted to leave Syria. The United States has gone through the process of peace negotiations and has failed because the Taliban are winning on the ground and are willing to give up little. Since we are unable to negotiate ourselves out of the war, this plan was devised: a huge battle that we can claim as the final victory that destroyed the Taliban. Under that guise, we can say that we have left the Afghan government in good shape. That will allow us to pack up and leave."

"But destroying this valley will not win the war," Aziz stated the obvious. "A year from now, a new harvest will be reaped and the drugs will flow again."

"You don't understand. This is going to be a show that won't have to be sold to the Afghans. The only people who will have to buy into it are the Americans. There will be media coverage unlike anything you have seen. US forces will leave behind a scorched valley and who knows how many dead people, but the show will allow us to leave."

"The United States is supposed to be a nation of values. You've spent nearly forty years preaching the goodness of your system over ours, when in the end you are no better than us. In the time you Americans have spent here, you have wasted both our time and your own time. You've preached that your system will free the world, when you have proven to be less honorable than the people you pretend to help."

"I understand all that, and you are right to feel that way, but I didn't come here to argue the good and bad of my government. I came to see you to try to prevent useless deaths. You said you and I have the power to avert this war. How?" The marine tried to redirect the conversation, knowing there was no way he could morally defend the actions of the United States. "The steady drip of blood has soured the American people, and only an Afghan bloodbath would make it seem our time here wasn't wasted. It is the same tactic that has been tried in every unwinnable war. It gives the side needing to escape the war a pathway out. If the marines were sent here as a triggering mechanism, how can I avoid tripping that trigger?"

"I intend to give the marines free run of the valley."

"Free run? What does that mean?"

"You will be ordered to run daily patrols. Do so with as many marines as you feel will get the job done, but use a large enough force to keep the smaller clans, with up to twenty fighters, at bay. While I control the major forces, the smaller groups are more radical and follow no one's orders but their own. The small armies will not attack a larger force and risk deaths that will reduce their numbers, and I will order our main forces to let you pass without engaging. If there is no bloodshed, there will be no justification to launch the air war."

"That's the tricky part." Santiago thought over what he had heard. "I don't know how long it is going to take for word of this plan to leak out to the press."

"Why don't you tell your press?"

"You have worked with the Americans long enough to know they play security games. This plan is highly classified. My giving the story to the press is against the law."

"Concentrate on saving lives. Then think about getting the story out." Aziz understood the obstacles that stood in the marine's way.

"The Americans are ready to leave your country. That can be seen in the way they are negotiating. They are doing so from a position of weakness. They want out of Afghanistan so badly that they have conceded to most of the demands the Taliban have made."

"Why don't they give into our last demand and let us take over the government?"

"Once we leave, it is assumed the Taliban will take over the government. This phony war is all about saving face. The United States has dumped nearly a trillion dollars into this failed war effort. They have lost nearly three thousand of their young people. It would be an embarrassment for them to admit defeat openly. With the pretense of a victory, we can rationalize that we received concessions that justify our pullout." Santiago hoped he was getting through to the Afghan. He understood that the marines and the Afghans in the valley were pawns in a game in which the chessboard was going to be slammed shut.

"You can't win on the battlefield, and you are desperate to leave my country, but you need something that will allow you to say that you won the final battle of the unwinnable war?" Aziz was amused by the thought. "You should never have come to my country. We have been fighting invaders for thousands of years. They have all left with a degree of humiliation, but only the Americans have the military power to destroy this valley."

"That's the big picture. Let's concentrate on our part." Santiago didn't want to get into the politics.

"I will have to run combat patrols. You have told me that the marines will be under surveillance of drones, and I assume satellites, to ensure we are following our instructions. Obviously, as we are being observed, enemy activity will be monitored. What the marines will need from you is for you to refrain from amassing your forces so that aerial imagery will not be able to direct the marines to them. If no enemy can be found, there will be no shots fired. Then maybe this whole crazy idea will have a chance to cool down."

"How long will this go on?"

"I don't know. The planning for this is being closely held in Washington, but as with all things in Washington, this secret will leak out. And then I'm sure the marines will be withdrawn from the valley."

"You ask a lot of me. When the CIA asks for favors, they usually pay. What is it that you can offer?"

"If we do this right, you might keep your brick plant intact and maybe still have a valley that is livable. I wish I could offer you more, but I can't."

"From your outposts, run your first patrols in the hills to the north. It will give me time reposition the forces I would have used against you."

"I'll request that the first patrol go north so that I can train the marines. I think I'll be allowed to do that."

"Within two days, I'll have my forces dispersed, but I have questions about how long this will have to go on. I can't allow my position to be weakened indefinitely."

Aziz fell silent, thinking about what he was committing to. "You won't be able to make another trip to visit me like you have today, but I'll find a way to communicate with you." Trying to lighten the mood, he said, "I don't usually get involved with crazy schemes. I should report you to the CIA and maybe earn a reward."

"That won't solve your problem. There is an entire air force poised to destroy you, your home, and your people. Having the CIA lock me up won't change that. If you want to take a chance, have your people kill me here. It would light the fuse that would make the valley glow red."

"You are the only American who has come to me able to speak to me in my language. I'm inclined to trust you for no rational reason, other than that you appear to be concerned with the human element in this war. Your people, my people, seem personal to you. They are flesh and blood, and you seem to want to prevent them from shedding anymore blood needlessly. You took a great risk in coming to me and asking me to take a chance on you. I will take that chance because I've seen the indiscriminate destruction your bombs cause."

Santiago was glad to hear the words, but he knew that somewhere in Aziz's concern for his people was his desire to save his business operation.

CHAPTER 4

THE BISHOP AND TRUTH

Santiago was in his bunker. When he was standing up, his head was barely at ground level, but his wasn't the only shelter constructed that way. All the marines lived as moles—and they lived that way day and night. The outposts set up were devoid of amenities. The nicety missed most was electricity. Nothing was lighted after the sun went down. Marines got to see with the use of night vision goggles. They were an advantage the Taliban didn't have, the darkened outposts being patches of ground the Taliban would have to probe in blackness.

After running patrols in the areas that Santiago had suggested before Washington took over the scheduling, it looked as if the truce he and Aziz had hastily agreed to would hold. Without the threat of losing their friends and having to run for their lives, the stress factor was taken off the marines, making them more able to tolerate the harsh conditions of living in the Stone Age. Of the dozens of patrols run, none had come under fire, and as those results were reported back to Washington, anxiety developed. It had been a week and no marines had been killed, while an entire air force was sitting on the ground awaiting orders to obliterate the Zukan.

"Sergeant Major," a lance corporal said, sticking his head into Santiago's hole in the ground, "there's a Brit trying to get into the encampment who says he wants to talk to you."

"Any idea how he got here?" Santiago was hoping the lance corporal would provide a guess that would turn out to be correct.

"He showed up in a white Toyota pickup."

Santiago smiled. It was the logical answer.

"Go get him and bring him to my conference room."

The lance corporal laughed. The conference room reference was a joke. Santiago had six boulders placed in a semicircle, and when he held meetings, most people stood because the rocks were too hard to sit on for anything longer than a minute.

Santiago observed from a distance as a strange-looking man was led to him. He was stout, and his large stomach was accentuated by his overly broad shoulders. His pinkish skin wasn't acclimated to the hot arid air and hadn't tanned like that of the natives. He seemed only to have gotten redder. As he walked up the slight rise, he removed his baseball cap and wiped beads of sweat from his bald head. He had hair, but it ringed a hairless crown and shot off at uncontrollable angles. As he put his hat back on, the hair dropped almost to his shoulders. Not only did he look unfit to be in the war zone but also he was unkempt, although this made it easy to discern his profession. Two cameras hung askew from his neck and bounced off his belly as he moved. He wore cargo shorts, and his exposed legs, unlike his florid face, were stark white, and so thin it was hard to imagine that they could support his bulk. Santiago couldn't see the man's arms, hidden under a long-sleeved shirt, but the entire picture was held together with a fisherman's vest with its myriad pockets stuffed with notebooks. There was no doubt that he was a reporter. And given the classification placed on what the marines were doing and the total press blackout thrown over the mission, he shouldn't have been there.

The sergeant major was curious. He didn't wait for his guest to arrive at the conference room. He moved down the hill to greet him.

Seeing the senior enlisted man, the reporter quickened his pace, reaching Santiago out of breath. Having to bend over to place his hands on his knees, he composed himself.

"Sergeant Major, I'm Nigel Bivens."

The introduction caught Santiago by surprise. The Englishman spoke in sonorous tones, almost Churchillian.

"Glad to meet you." Santiago stuck out his hand.

"You're a hard man to get to. You Americans usually facilitate reporters visiting the troops because we write eloquent stories about the US effort."

"Perhaps someone thought you might not write a good story this time."

"Why would that be?"

Santiago led him to the stone circle, where he offered him a rock seat.

Bivens, unlike others who had sat there previously, didn't wince. He seemed glad to be taking a load off his feet.

"I'm curious. You surely know there is a blanket press ban associated with this mission. What the hell you are doing here?"

"Good question. But before I answer, do you mind if I have a pick-me-up? It's been a long day." Bivens took a flask from an inner pocket of his vest and offered the marine a drink.

"No, thank you, but you go ahead."

With the marine's approval, Bivens took a long, hard swallow. "I find that a spot of alcohol helps me organize my thoughts." Without asking, he took out an Afghan rolled cigarette and lit up. After he'd taken a long inhale, the exhalation seemed even longer.

"My questions still hold. How did you get here? Why are you here?"

"I'll answer the second question first." Bivens was nonplussed. "With the war winding down and you Americans pulling back wherever you can, there aren't many stories to write—and that's how

I make my living. When, all of a sudden, a marine unit is deployed to a place where there is no winning, I smell a story. I also smell a story in the way these outposts were named. There is nothing in US history that would allow for outposts to be named as these are. Gabrielle, Anne Marie, and Claudine are not names associated with US war efforts."

Santiago in that instant knew Bivens had locked onto the message he'd been trying to send.

"The last time those names were used was by the French before they lost their empire in Indo-China. Is that the message you're trying to send with the naming of the outposts? As I looked around coming here, I saw that the clumps of marines you've positioned are really too close to be called outposts. They are merely forward areas of your camp. I'm wondering if the names are supposed to send a dispatch that the world hasn't picked up on yet?"

"Don't read anything into them. When we arrived here, I set up a naming contest, thinking the marines would have fun with it. The winner was a marine of French descent. He picked the names."

"Sergeant Major, with all due respect, don't bullshit a bullshitter."

"Nigel, you've shown up here, an area that is under a total press blackout, and you're asking for answers that are beyond any classification you might have."

"You're correct. I have no classification. I've been freelancing this war for ten years. You see, I was going to follow my hero Winston Churchill by becoming a war correspondent and returning home to change the face of Britain. The flaw in my plan was that, unlike with his war, no one in Britain gives a shit about Afghanistan. And I have no family connections to propel me forward. I'm stuck here in a war my countrymen don't read about and with not enough money to buy me entrée into society. That said, some of the big Western wire services buy my work output, but I basically work for Al Jazeera. They like my stuff because I self-edit and they can usually run with the stories I submit. As it turns out, Al Jazeera is the only honest news broker of this war. To use an American expression, they tell it like it is, and therefore they are kept at arm's length, because no one in the United States wants to read the truth. Besides, they pay well, and since I really have no place to go, here I am."

"How have you survived? Running around by yourself in a pickup truck can't be healthy."

"It's a bit of a thrill, but I speak Pashto, and that allows me to talk myself out of tight places—sometimes. That, and I have written favorable stories about some of the Afghan powerbrokers. I think that this, more than anything, is the key. Even though we consider these people just beyond the Iron Age, they like to read about themselves."

Santiago tested him and asked him a question in Pashto, which Bivens answered.

"Sergeant Major"—he returned to English—"you are a surprising man. I have only met several Americans who spoke the language of the people they have been sent here to help, and they have all been interpreters. Obviously, you're self-taught, because if you had gone through the military schools, you'd be an interpreter." Bivens looked over the man he was speaking to, seeing him in a different light for the first time. "I find you interesting. An enlisted man in charge of a company-sized unit with a mission to which no one will attest who is maintaining the cloak of secrecy while sending out a message for the world to read loud and clear. Anyone with half a brain can see that by naming the outposts as you have, you are trying to wake up those in power. Unfortunately, no one is listening. I think you need me."

"You've explained why you're here, but you haven't answered how you got here. The Zukan is usually closed to outsiders."

"That is where my superb writing comes in. I did several stories on Aziz, and he has pretty much given me safe passage. You see, like you, I know he is the power in this valley. It was he who told me that you would have a story for me. I think you impressed him when you met."

"He told you that we met?"

"Yes."

"What else did he say?" Santiago was concerned. He'd wanted the meeting to remained undetected.

"Aziz offers no information other than that which suits his purposes. It suited his purpose that I should meet you, so I'm here. And good or bad, I can smell a story." Bivens was sure of himself.

"You're wrong. There is no story here." Santiago was glad the Englishman was on the scent. Someone had to get the news to the US public because the standoff with Aziz and the destruction of the valley couldn't be put off indefinitely.

"If it is okay with you, Sergeant Major, I'd like to talk to the French marine who named the outposts. He must be a student of military history, as am I."

Santiago, not having expected the request, stalled. "He's out on patrol and won't be back until tonight. And I can't have you in the camp at night. There is no place to put you."

"Sergeant Major, again, with all due respect, that answer doesn't hold water. I'm guessing that you are Private Frenchie." Bivens was sure of his assertion.

Santiago wasn't angry at being caught in a lie. He guessed that Bivens was a bloodhound that, once on the scent of a story, wasn't going to let it go. He was also thinking about how he could use the only pressman within a hundred miles.

"You don't have to make up a lie. Your long delay tells me all I need to know. I'll make your job easy. Give me access to the camp for the day, and I'll write up my story so that you can read it and make any corrections needed. You can be the final filter in editing out things that are classified, because as I talk to the marines, I'm sure some are going to expose secrets. Will you allow me to do that?"

Santiago paused, as if he was thinking about denying the request, and tried not to show his happiness that Bivens was willing to get the marines' story out.

Bivens wrote his story based on what he'd heard from the marines and what he thought the plan for them was. Al Jazeera published it in the Arab world, but it seeped into the Western media's consciousness. On a slow news Saturday, the *Washington Post* ran Bivens's article uncut, except for space requirements, and the staffers working in the White House knew that the story portended bad days ahead. Stanley Weeks was informed that the top secret mission was laid out for all to see. His first cover-your-ass action was to call the president.

Reaching Baron on the golf course and interrupting his game was not what Weeks wanted to do, but he needed guidance.

"Mr. President," he spoke calmly, "it appears that we have had a breach in our security for Angel Fire." He used the code name for the mission, which Baron thought signified divine intervention from the sky. "Most of the details have been laid out in a *Washington Post* article."

Weeks expected the response. Baron's anger wasn't over the fact that the mission was exposed or that it was inferred that the marines were expendable. He wanted the name of the reporter who'd broken the story. He would seek revenge there.

"Sir, the story wasn't reported by any of the fake media reporters. It was broken by an Al Jazeera stringer."

"What the hell is that?"

"It's a Qatari news service." Weeks didn't know exactly what Al Jazeera was, but he did know they were involved with the news on all platforms.

"Qatari? Get on the phone with their ambassador and tell him I want to talk to him."

"What would be a good time for you, sir?"

"I don't want my weekend interrupted. Set it up for Monday."

"Yes, sir."

The ambassador was out of town, so a meeting could not be scheduled before Wednesday. Weeks assembled his brain trust. They were shocked that a parallel could be so easily drawn between the

Zukan and Dien Bien Phu. They were also sure that the US public wouldn't know of the failed French effort. But having Angel Fire referenced as a replay of that doomed mission was sure to rouse some interest among the US media.

"What a fucking mess." Weeks summed up the feeling of his group. "We're going to have to brief the president, but we'll play down the French references. We can't let it be known that we failed to mention the French effort when we briefed him. We'll up-brief the differences in the plans and play heavily on our total superiority in airpower. We'll have to try to explain why the marines haven't been able to draw the Taliban into a fight. We know they have been patrolling and looking for the Taliban, who seem to have disappeared. We might recommend that we reduce the size of the marine force so that the Taliban will be sure they can overrun it." Weeks was trying to think of solutions on the fly, but he had no idea what the president might listen to.

He arrived at the Oval Office with the people who had sold Angel Fire.

"How'd this thing get so fucked up?" The president accused the NSC personnel as they entered the office, taking the starch out of their spines.

"Would you please tell me what a foreign reporter is doing nosing around in our business? I thought we had classified this so that no one would know what was going on. We still have a press blackout, don't we?" His words slammed into the staffers.

Weeks, knowing that he had to respond, did so in a murmur: "From what we could find out, the reporter in question is a freelancer who'll write stories for anyone who will buy them. Apparently, Al Jazeera bought this one."

"How could he have equated this with the French thing?" The president didn't know himself about the French in Vietnam.

"Apparently, a marine private named the outposts after his ex-girlfriends, and the names were the same as the outposts the French named in Vietnam. It was an odd coincidence."

"Get rid of that marine. I don't like coincidences." The office went silent. The staff, not wanting to add any fuel to the fire they could see consuming the president, waited for him to guide them through their next actions.

"I was playing golf with Erik King when you called. You know him; he runs ISSAC. He was telling me that he has about five thousand people in Afghanistan providing security services all around the country. He thinks the marines are not being aggressive enough in seeking out the Taliban."

"They run combat patrols several times a day, and the Taliban avoid them." Weeks couldn't believe the president had discussed a plan that he wanted classified with a civilian.

"He thinks there are too many marines on the ground and they are scaring the Taliban away. He suggests a small security force could pick a fight and get this whole thing started in a couple of days. What do you think?"

Weeks was loath to tell Baron that it was a bad idea, but he could see that the president had latched onto it. He liked ideas where he could funnel money to friends. "Do you want me to coordinate actions between Mr. King and the marines?"

"No. Let me think about it. And if I decide to use security contractors, I'll handle it."

The National Security Council staff knew they were going to be cut out of whatever Baron and King decided. That was evidenced when Weeks received a call from the Defense Department requesting clarification on why contractors were being sent to the Zukan. While the contractors were under a contract to the DoD, the military had no control of them. They were immune from military guidance and were the ones to do the menial jobs the military was glad to farm out. In Afghanistan, most of their security work was done to protect politically connected Afghans, so when the DoD, who was paying them, asked them to do something, they refused under the guise that they were contracted to Afghans. The same scam worked in reverse. When the Afghans asked them to do certain jobs, they said they couldn't because they were DoD contractors. As a result of the clouded conditions under which they worked, they were freelancers carrying shiny weapons, making big money, and controlled only by a shadowy network of men tied to the upper levels of government.

When King received an early morning phone call, he didn't have to hear the words Baron used to rationalize his decision. He knew what had to be done. Without informing the DoD or the Afghans, he got word to his people in Kabul. That was all it took. There was no government red tape. The final battle of the war would be put into play by civilian contractors from Xyze, the security branch of the ISSAC Company.

Santiago was unaware of the arrival of twelve Americans in the valley. The news was brought to him by Bivens. The Englishman had no idea why the Taliban had left the marines alone, but he knew the arrival of a group he described as gunslingers wasn't a positive sign.

"Sergeant Major, what happened? Did you marines need help?"

"What are you talking about?" Santiago had become friendly with the Englishman. Their conversations usually started with teasing.

"Your American handlers mustn't be happy with the job you're doing, so they are going to assist you. I think they have sent contractors here to save you."

"Nigel, take a deep breath, compose yourself, and tell me what you are trying to say without hyperventilating." Santiago was amused.

"Mind if I light up?" he asked as if they were in an enclosed box rather than standing on a treeless hillock. He pulled out a fat black cigar and lit it.

"That's very Churchillian," the marine joked.

"Well, if I can't become my hero, I can at least emulate him." He exhaled an unhealthy plume of smoke.

"So, you have something to tell me. What is it?"

"Americans love action, and my guess is that some of your decision makers got tired of the slow pace at which you are pursuing the Taliban. Your patrolling and finding no Taliban to engage doesn't make for a good video game. My guess is that some real war fighters have been sent to stir the pot and get this little war going."

"And you base that on what?" Santiago wanted more information.

"Yesterday a dozen American security contractors who are supposed to be part of the group protecting the Afghan government leaders leased a compound on the outskirts of Naaz from Aziz. He was concerned enough about their arrival that he brought me in and wanted me to ask you what you thought was going on. He doesn't like the idea that there are freelancers in the province, and he wonders why they're here. He is upset that neither you nor his CIA friends told him this was coming."

"Why did he let them in? He could have refused to rent them anything."

"You forget, Aziz is first and foremost a businessman, one who will be here long after we are gone. Money motivates him, and the new arrivals paid well. Besides, he thinks he can control them."

Santiago accepted the businessman part of the explanation, but he thought Aziz was overestimating his ability to control the contractors. "Can you take me to the compound they rented?" he asked Bivens.

"Of course. I relish being in the middle of a mystery."

"You may not like this one."

"You're wrong. I've already got this story mapped out. As soon as you meet with the new arrivals and give me the nod, I'll blow the lid off this ploy. Sergeant Major, I'm glad I found you. You're going to get me a journalistic prize because I am going to sweep all the American reporters."

"Either that or you're going to take a bullet," Santiago joked, informing Bivens that his expectation might be arrived at with peril.

They drove to Naaz in Bivens's beat-up pickup, which Santiago discovered was less comfortable than riding in a Hummer. The rented compound was separated from the town by half a mile and stood alone. Santiago looked over the building complex with a military eye and saw that to the inexperienced it looked secure from ground attack, but it sat below the mountains, where he knew mortar pits were dug in. The compound was an easy mark for mortar fire. The walls surrounding the compound would protect those inside from gunfire, but the place was in a perilous position and susceptible to overhead fire. Confirming his thoughts were several craters caused by previous mortar attacks that had partially grown over. They indicated that the compound was preregistered for the mountain mortars. That wasn't his problem. He worried that the new arrivals had the potential of throwing off the balance of forces in the valley.

"I think you'd better wait in the truck," he instructed Bivens. "I'm going to try to get information from them, and they might not talk in front of you. I'll give you a full brief on the drive back to the encampment."

"Which one, Eagle, Raven, or Condor?" Bivens laughed at the idea that a presidential order had been issued to change the names of the outposts, but it was too late to prevent the idea that the project in the Zukan was doomed to the same fate as the French debacle.

"I like Gabrielle." Santiago laughed as he exited the vehicle.

He didn't know what to expect, but he was surprised to find that people who sold themselves as security experts had no security in place. While the contractors he could see looked hard core, there was no secure entry point, so he walked into a courtyard between the buildings. The men he found were heavily armed, sporting assault rifles manufactured throughout the world that they weren't bashful about displaying as a sign of their power. The weaponry the contractors wore was like a scene from the Old West. Bandoliers crossed their bodies, indicating that each man carried enough firepower to make him self-sufficient on the battlefield. The other accoutrements, besides the weapons, were reflector sunglasses. Each man walked around menacingly. Santiago wondered about the glasses and if they were worn to hide the fear that might be emanating from the men's eyes.

"Can you tell me where I might find your boss?" he asked a contractor once he was well inside what should have been their guarded perimeter.

He received a disdainful look. The contractors looked down on the military. They were the ones doing the dirty work in Afghanistan, and they weren't making any money at it. It was obvious the contractors had given up on the notion of duty. Money was the new god.

"Yeah. Dave Morey should be in that building," one of the contractors directed the marine.

Santiago, following the directions given, entered a windowless room where two men were stretched out on cots. Both were fully armed even in repose.

"Dave Morey?" Santiago directed the question at both men.

"Yeah." One moved enough to throw his legs over the side of the cot and sit up. "Who's looking for me?" He took a while to stand.

"I'm Sergeant Major Santiago. I'm commanding the marine unit in the valley."

"You're the guy." Morey was snide. "We're here to do your job." He was used to dealing with men with titles, and it was apparent he considered talking to an enlisted man to be beneath him.

"I wasn't aware the marines needed help in doing the job."

"Yeah, well somebody, like the president, thinks you need help. We'll show you how to gin up a war." Morey had been a captain in the army and was released from active duty under questionable circumstances. He had hooked up with Xyze and had worked for them for ten years. Carrying guns without the need for a physical regiment had softened him. It was difficult to tell his girth because he was wrapped in body armor and had bandoliers and guns draping off him. His puffy face had begun to jowl into his neck, indicating a softness that didn't equate to conditioning required on the battlefield. It was impossible to see his eyes because even in the darkened room he wore his reflector sunglasses, but they couldn't hide his nose, which hooked downward toward perpetually sneering tight lips.

"Well, now that you're here to help the marines, maybe we can help you."

"I doubt it." Morey considered himself above listening to an enlisted man, especially a sergeant major, someone who had made a career out of the military and had passed up the big money.

Santiago was not put off by the attitude. "Even if you succeed in ginning up your war, the location you've chosen is vulnerable and will be taken out in the first hours."

"What are you talking about?"

"You sit under hills that are ringed with mortar pits. My guess would be that this compound is preregistered and will destroyed. That is probably why Aziz let you have it. If you remain here, you unfortunately will be taken out." Santiago delighted in pointing out the obvious that was missed by the supposed experts. "I'd recommend that you move to the marine encampment. We're pretty much covered from overhead fire." The purpose of the sergeant major's suggestion was twofold: he was willing to protect Americans whom he thought were in over their heads, and if he could get these contractors into the marine encampment, he could control them.

"I'm a former captain of artillery. I know about overhead fires. I don't need an enlisted man telling me about them. We'll handle the situation from here. We've seen your place; it's not suitable for us. We live above ground."

Santiago summed up the situation and wouldn't argue further. "I think it would be a good idea if we coordinated our operations. We don't want to end up shooting one another."

"Sergeant Major, perhaps I didn't make myself clear. We are here to do a job. We don't need marine help, and we don't need coordination. We run our own show. You'd be smart to stay out of our way. We're professionals, the guys called in to mop up your mess. Now do you understand?"

"Good luck. But if I were you, I'd set up some security at the gate. Anyone can walk in here. Who knows, someone might bring the war to you." Santiago realized that he hadn't gotten through to Morey and that no amount of reasoning would. The contractor was on an ego high, relishing the thought of doing the job the marines couldn't.

"How'd it go?" Bivens asked as the marine returned to his truck.

"Drive, and I'll give you the full rundown." Santiago took a deep breath to calm himself before briefing the Englishman.

"Nigel, do you think you can run a story about the marines being displaced by mercenaries, something that will pull on the heartstrings of the public?"

"I'm glad you asked, because while you were talking to the contractors, I tried to figure out why they were here. I sat in the truck and wrote this." He handed Santiago a notebook with barely legible pencil markings. "Tell me if that is what you had in mind."

<hr>

The president received a late-night call from a Fox News confidant, Sean Harris, that the United States had displaced the marines in Zukan and replaced them with paid contractors. Harris wanted confirmation. The news channel was going to bury the story, but they wanted to have a cover story in place when other media broke it.

"How in the hell did this get out? It was a deal I set up with Erik King. No one in the government has any idea what we are doing," the president complained. He knew the talking head on the phone was a friend and wouldn't betray his confidence as Baron expressed his anger.

"It looks like the same Al Jazeera reporter is running around and getting stories that you wanted blacked out in the US media."

"I purposely had the US media cut off from this, and I want this Al Jazeera guy cut off too. There has to be some way to cut this guy off. Maybe Erik can have one of his people on-site silence this guy," the president mused.

"That's a bad idea. I'm going to forget what you just said; you're getting into dangerous territory." The Fox opinion maker wanted no knowledge of what the president might do.

"Don't worry, Sean. This will all be done outside of government channels. Erik knows how to do things like this."

"Mr. President, I want to caution you about taking that course of action. If it should ever get out that you authorized an assassination of a newsman, there will be hell to pay."

"It will be the removal of a national security threat. I have the power to do that."

Harris had to divert the president and, while he was distracted, end the conversation. There was no telling what would trigger his getting back to the talk of taking out Nigel Bivens.

"You're rally last week was great. It looked like the people loved you making your reelection a snap."

It worked. There was no more talk of an assassination. Baron jumped to his favorite topic: himself.

"Yeah, I didn't use the teleprompter, and that pissed off my staff, but I thought my riffs were great. The audience loved them."

"They sure did, Mr. President." Harris spoke as if he were talking a suicidal jumper back from the ledge.

"You know the southern crowds like a lot of God talk. How'd you like the part about the sanctity of life that I gave them? My religious supporters loved that. I can say anything, and they believe it. Did you see the crowd when I laid on the value of each fetus? There wasn't a dry eye in the house."

"You're doing great, Mr. President, so I'll talk to you tomorrow." Harris knew his fortunes were tied to the president, but he wondered if he was locked in a Faustian bargain. There was no telling when Baron might go over the edge and take his supporters with him.

———

Bivens's story seeped into US media. Santiago was astonished to learn that it hadn't been given full play. He was dumbfounded that the US media didn't want the story of mercenaries with the potential of leading the country into a wider war for no reason other than to give the president a bargaining chip to escape the mess the United States had created. In all the discussions about the air war and how it would play on TV, no one had given thought to the hundreds of Afghans who were going to die. They focused on the shiny object. The hot topic was Private Frenchie and how he had coincidently named the outposts for his girlfriends. No one cared that Dien Bien Phu was a disaster for the troops on the ground. They all wanted to know the names of Frenchie's girlfriends so they could interview them. The people Bivens's story roused were the contractors who worked for Xyze.

Morey, the former captain of artillery, who didn't need the help of an enlisted man, showed up at the marine camp seeking help. As a man coming for a favor, he couldn't humble himself. His attitude was that war was a moneymaking operation and that those who fought wars for the nebulous concepts of duty and honor were saps. When he entered Santiago's mole hole, where the sergeant major's sleeping bag and air mattress were on the ground, he was more convinced of his views.

Barely able to see in the unlighted underground bunker, he took the small camping stool Santiago offered him. The sergeant major sat across from him with their knees touching. The closeness made Morey uncomfortable, but he had come for a reason.

"I'm going to need a detail of marines to protect our compound." He spoke as if he had the right to order marines.

"I don't have the personnel to spare." The sergeant major was matter-of-fact. He barely had enough manpower to protect the ground they occupied.

"I need marines to provide security for my men."

"I thought you were the security experts." Santiago couldn't help himself. He had to get the dig in.

"We're the best, but we're undermanned. I need your marines to protect my people."

"That seems to be a personal problem. You've got thousands of security contractors running around the country. Why don't you request support from your company?"

"That's not the way it works. Low-priced help is supposed to protect us."

"Not this low-priced help. We don't have anyone to spare." Santiago was amused. "As I see it, you have two options. You can go through your company and get more help, or you can move into the camp with the marines."

"I could take this to DoD, and they could order you to provide assistance." Morey had no intention of moving out of his aboveground accommodations to live in the dirt.

Santiago guessed that his guest wouldn't have been in his camp requesting assistance if he could have taken another route. He was stuck. Xyze had sent his team to the valley to do a job after estimating the cost per contractor and figured twelve would be sufficient. For Morey to come up on the wire and ask for more help would make the Xyze auditors angry. He was boxed in and had only the marines to bail him out.

"That's your prerogative. When I receive orders, I'll see what I can spare."

"We're Americans fighting the same war with the same ends. You should feel honored that I'm asking for your help in this joint venture."

"My goal is to keep marines alive, and your job is to stir things up and probably get some killed. You're asking me to sacrifice marines to protect you as you deliver on a project that you're in over your head on. I cautioned you previously about your need for security, which you blew off, only to find out you do need ground security. I'll caution you to be careful in seeking a fight in this valley because I doubt that you or your team will survive one."

"We'll do all right," Morey spoke with arrogance.

"Since you won't help me with security, I need to know if you've ever seen this English reporter who works for that Arab propaganda outfit Al Jazeera. People in Washington think he's becoming a national security threat, so if any marines see him, grab him and hold him until I can talk to him."

"I don't know what you're talking about," Santiago lied. "There are no reporters around here."

"No one has figured out how he gets around and gets his stories, but he ain't doing our effort in Afghanistan any good."

"We're on a press blackout for this mission, and no reporter has breached our gate security."

"Well, the son of a bitch is getting information somehow. He got the Private Frenchie story from the marines."

"Yeah, that's what I heard, but I have canvassed every marine, and none of them has had contact with him. He must have made his story up."

"Well, somehow he got the story about what we have come here to do, and it isn't sitting well with the bosses of my company. So if you should see him nosing around, grab him."

Morey was through. He stood to leave. Even with being as short as he was, he could not stand upright in the sergeant major's lair. Hitting his head, he was angry. He had had enough of the marines.

———

Had Dave Morey been aware of his surroundings, he would have seen Bivens's truck parked close to the vehicle he had driven to the marine camp. The Englishman was living with the marines. He had received word that he was a marked man, slated to be eliminated if Xyze contractors ever got to him. No one bothered to look at how journalists died or at the fact that only a few were killed in firefights or accidental bombings. Most were killed because people in power, people who felt threatened, eliminated them. It was so easy to do under the guise of war. They became collateral damage that wasn't talked about. Bivens knew the statistics, so when he discovered that the security contractors were looking for him, he sought the marines' help.

Morey's mood was not helped when he returned to the security contractors' compound. He hadn't had time to take off his armored vest when his satellite phone beeped. The tone was alarming. He had never answered the phone to receive good news, but he couldn't ignore the call because he was required to have the phone with him at all times.

"Morey here," he answered dourly.

"Hang on a minute," the voice on the phone instructed. "We're patching you through to Washington."

In all his time working for Xyze, he had never talked to anyone from Washington. He used to joke that that was above his pay grade. Now, apparently, he was at that level.

"Who am I talking to?" The voice was gruff, no-nonsense.

"This is Dave Morey."

"This is Erik King." The name was enough to identify him. "Dave, we have a problem, and that means you have a problem. I promised the president our guys could do what the marines couldn't. To that end, you were sent to your location to find a pretext so that we could get the Taliban into a fight and get on with the war. When you took the job, you assured your bosses on-site in Afghanistan that you could handle what you were sent to do, but you haven't done shit. All we are getting are reports about how badly things are screwed up. It's making us look bad. It's making me look bad." King got to the crux of his anger. "I told the president we could get a fight going. I just got off the phone with him. He isn't happy with our performance. Now, I'm not going to sugarcoat this. You either do what you were sent to do within the next couple of days or I'll terminate all your contracts and you can go looking for other jobs. Is that clear enough?"

"Yes, sir."

"Good. Now let's talk about the other job you were assigned. There is another article in this morning's papers by the English reporter. Find the son of a bitch and find some guise for removing him. He's laying out what is a top secret plan. That is impinging on our national security." King laid out the flimsy reasoning condoning Bivens' removal. "He's a national security threat and has to go. Can you make that happen?"

"I've got a couple of men tracking him down. He won't be a threat much longer."

"That's good, but make it quick, because if he continues to report, he is going to blow the lid off this. And then all our efforts will have been for naught. Am I clear enough for you?"

"Yes, sir." Dave Morey didn't like being scolded by anyone, even the head of the company. The harsh words hurt him. He was grateful when the call ended.

Not one to suffer alone, Morey called his group together in a building they used as a meeting area. All arrived armed and looking dangerous. They displayed an attitude that they were the best at what they did. What they hadn't done irked him.

With most sitting slouched over chairs, a few stood against the walls with their weapons ready and their fingers on the triggers.

"I just got my ass chewed out by Erik King." The mention of the name drew everyone's attention, because when the boss called, it wasn't usually good news. "He's in communication with the president, and they are pissed that we haven't accomplished shit. We were supposed to kick some Taliban ass, and it hasn't happened. From today forward, we are going to become more aggressive. If the Taliban won't pick a fight with us, we'll tear up some of the opium crops to goad them into a fight. We'll do anything we have to. We've got to figure out some way to get them into a fight. Have any of you got any ideas on something that might work?"

"What the hell are the marines doing?" someone offered.

"Forget about the marines. They are having as much luck getting the Taliban to attack as we've had. The only difference is that they aren't making the big bucks to get this thing going like we are. We were sent here as the professionals, rainmakers, so tomorrow our rules of engagement change. We will attack any perceived threat."

"What should we consider a perceived threat?" someone asked.

"I don't know," Morey confessed. "We'll know one when we see one. If we see anyone carrying a weapon, that will be enough to take them down. If we build a body count, I'm sure the Taliban will come after us. Then we can kick the shit out of them. That should appease the boss, and show we've done something to earn the bonuses we are receiving for being assigned this job." Morey waited for questions. When none came, he started in on the second gripe King had related to him. "There's an English reporter somewhere in this valley who is reporting on what's happening here."

"Isn't that what reporters are supposed to do?" Someone tried to lighten the mood of the group.

"He's not painting a good picture of us. In fact, he's making us look bad." Morey wasn't amused. "He is considered a national security risk, so his killing would be covered under national security regulations." Morey didn't know if what he had said was correct, but he wanted to ease the consciences of the group. They would kill for money, but with the national security rationale, they could do so thinking they were acting legitimately. "For the person who bags his pelt, there'll be a bonus of twenty grand. If a team gets him, the bonus money will be divided in equal parts."

"We've done a lot of extralegal shit over here, but murdering a European isn't the same as killing rag heads. I don't think any of us signed on to do something like that." A voice of dissent rose from the group. "Say we take this guy out and word somehow leaks to the Brits. They are going to raise hell and want answers and a fall guy. Who, in that event, is going to cover us? This isn't something that will be swept under the rug as easily as it would be if it were another Afghan. Any defense we were to offer that we had shot an enemy would be blown away. Who's going to foot the bill if this goes to trial?"

"Don't worry about it. We'll be covered," Morey said, having his own doubts.

"Which job do you want done first?"

"We can scour the valley for the Englishman while looking for opportunities to hit the Afghans. We'll multitask. We're professionals. We can do that." Morey was trying to motivate his team as he sensed their enthusiasm flagging.

"You made an important omission," a voice came from the group. "You just said 'hit the Afghans.' I signed on for this to hit the Taliban. Are you saying we have license to hit any target?"

Morey didn't like being pinned down. If he changed the mission to engaging Afghans, he was exceeding what he had been sent to do, but he felt boxed in. King wanted action, and if the Taliban wouldn't engage, he was going to have to open the scope of his job. "Any perceived threat is okay. It doesn't have to be the Taliban." As he muttered the words, he realized he had taken a step that might be beyond his authority, but he wanted to do something to look good in his boss's eyes.

Xyze personnel left their compound looking for a fight as Morey had channeled the anger of Erik King. They didn't know exactly what they were looking for; they only guessed they would recognize a perceived threat. They rode through the village of Bada, in the heart of the opium trade, staying on the hard-surfaced roads US money had built. They never used roads that were not trafficked because of the threat of explosive devices embedded in such seldom-used roads. They left all the off-road patrolling to the marines because none of the contractors wanted to return home missing limbs. The difficulty in what they were trying to do was evident. They were looking for a fight in a place where people engaged in commerce, and while weapons were occasionally seen, they were the gear of men trying to ensure there were no thefts.

In a frustrating day, none of the twelve-man Xyze team could conjure anything that could be considered a threat. Returning to their compound, Morey was frantic. When Erik King wanted something done, he wanted it done now. He was paying his contractors well to accomplish his aims and wouldn't accept excuses. Morey had nothing to report on what he and his team considered his orders, and they were angry about it, not understanding why they couldn't find something or someone one to shoot. They rationalized their failure and how it was going to play out at corporate headquarters, understanding there was a real chance that they might be replaced by another team.

"Okay," Morey spoke to the disgruntled group. "We fucked up today, but I'm going to cover for us. I'm going to report that we made contact with a group of about ten Taliban and say that in the encounter, shots were fired until they retreated. I'm going to say we have a good idea of their location and tomorrow we will set a trap for them. That, I think, will buy us time, but it only buys us another day. Tomorrow we have to make it rain because we are on a short leash. Erik has apparently sold the president on the idea that Xyze can do what the military can't. Any questions?"

By placing the onus on the team members, Morey hoped to frighten them with the implication of threatened job security. No one wanted to be replaced and lose the bonus money they would make if they could start a war.

"Bada isn't a place where we are going to find the Taliban, at least not any who will come out and engage us. We are going to have to take a chance and hit some of these outlying villages that aren't as heavily engaged in the opium trade," a team member offered.

"Screw that," another team member rebutted. "If we get into the hinterland, we will be exposing ourselves to an IED threat. And I didn't sign on for this to get blown up. I'd just as soon give up the bonus money than take a chance on getting maimed."

Several in the group were of the same mind. They nodded in agreement.

Morey, able to see his group splintering, had to say something that would keep them together. "There's a way to do this without exposing ourselves to danger. We stick to the main roads like we did today, but tomorrow we'll push through Bada and go out to Kuk. It's a shit village, but the road through it handles a lot of truck traffic, so it should be a safe ride. We'll leave the vehicles and walk streets that we know have had foot traffic. They should be IED-clear. I expect that the people in Kuk have never seen an armed group other than the Taliban, so we'll probably receive resistance. If we do, we'll take out as many people as we can and then withdraw. I think that will be enough to make the higher-ups happy. It will also give them the story that will allow them to commence the big war. If we play this right, everyone on our side walks away happy. When we get back here tomorrow, I'll call in the helicopter, and we'll be back in Kabul when the shit hits the fan. You guys buy into that?" Morey spoke to the group he considered dissidents.

"What about the reporter? You can't paper that over with bullshit," a voice said to try to get an explanation for the other part of their mission.

"We don't do national security threats. That's the CIA's job. After we clear out, they can come in and take care of it."

"How about the bonus money?"

"Getting the war started will be enough pay for me." Morey had evidently lowered his expectations. "I think in this instance we'd better be ready to settle for a half loaf."

Receiving the nodded approval from the majority of the team, Morey walked off alone. He needed to think about the day's failure and how he was going to sell that to corporate. Knowing he was on the cusp of losing the bonus his group had been promised, he was resolved that they would earn it the following day. He tried to envision what he could claim as a threat in Kuk.

Kuk had been chosen because it was the end of the road, literally. US money had run out and the paved road ended, but it fed into a spiderweb of dirt roads that headed to the hills in all directions. At the end of the Zukan Valley, the flat expanse of earth was a prime poppy-growing area that fed its product into the normal drug traffic, but because it was at the end of the road, there was a loose alliance between the local farmers and the drug bundlers who bought the product. That left room for the locals to use the network of dirt roads to cut side deals with small buyers who came from Pakistan. The Aziz network allowed the skimming because the local farmers were feeding markets that outdistanced their ability to serve. Kuk was the "Wild West," a frontier town that hadn't yet been incorporated in the major drug trade. Farmers made their own deals with buyers who seemed to descend out of the mountains.

Unlike other towns that were laid out on a grid and where streets were defined, Kuk had no organization. It was as if several hundred huts had fallen out of the sky and risen randomly from the parched soil. There was no way to get through the village in a straight line.

The Xyze contractors worried about the layout and what they might find, but they followed the same routine as the previous day. Three-man teams climbed into four pickup trucks rented to them by Aziz. Morey rode in the lead vehicle with two men, Bill Rapp and Charlie Drew, whom he knew were of like mind. They were a part of the team of men who wouldn't hesitate to pull the trigger. Morey hadn't known them before taking them on, but he hired them based on the reputations they had gained in Kabul. They were men who were always looking for a fight and a chance to use their weapons. They came from dissimilar backgrounds. No one at Xyze had vetted them too closely. Rapp, a small man who always seemed to be punching above his weight, lived with an inferiority complex. The only way he could overcome his perceived weaknesses was with a gun. It gave him power. He looked for work where he could carry his power. He had applied to work for the local sheriff and was sent off to the state's police academy, where he was a bust.

It was determined he was too aggressive, so he was released from the school. Upon his return to his hometown, the only job he could find where he was allowed to wear a gun was as a mall security guard. It was a comedown, but as he walked the mall with a gun on his hip, he did so with an aura of omnipotence. He wasn't sure if people were looking at him or at the gun, but he relished the idea that when he walked around the mall, people parted before him like the sea in the Bible. Even during his time off, he wore a weapon concealed, feeling no one could touch him because he had the power of the gun. It was a coincidence that a high school friend who had been an army ranger met him in the mall and struck up a conversation. His friend had received a job offer from Xyze to go back to Afghanistan and do safer work than he had been doing as a soldier—and for a lot more money. The story enthralled Rapp. He called the contact numbers at Xyze that his friend had given him. He polished up his résumé so there was no mention of the failed police training. Xyze hired him as a security contractor. He saw immediately the power that guns gave him in Afghanistan, and he armored up with the best weapons money could buy. The shiny guns changed him. He became vocal in his hatred for the Afghans. He talked often about killing them. His wild fantasies grew until people who knew him thought he had slipped a gear and had become someone he wasn't. It was based on his reputation as a hard charger that Morey had wanted him on his team, thinking he would be a good man to have near.

Charlie Drew was a good-looking blond-haired former police officer standing at six foot three who had soured in his job. As he dealt with more people whom he considered the dregs of the earth, he became more cynical and frightened that every call or traffic stop boded danger. The feeling overwhelmed him, which was why his gun was always out of its holster, threatening citizens. His conduct became so aggressive that he was dismissed for use of excessive force. In letting him go, the police department for which he worked, not wanting to tarnish his chance at further employment, wrote him glowing reports. With Drew's reputation not following him, Xyze thought they had found a winner. As his past was whitewashed, his cynicism grew. He became paranoid in a war zone where the enemy used unconventional warfare, and he saw an enemy in every Afghan. He couldn't sleep. His obsession grew. Among a group of security contractors who all had a degree of distrust for the Afghan population, his stated hatred of the Afghans didn't turn other contractors off; they felt the same as he did. Being vocal, Drew was considered a leader by men who remained silent. Morey had heard of him and wanted him on his team.

As they walked the lanes and paths of Kuk without success, Morey's anxiety grew. The contractors had gone back to their trucks and repositioned themselves several times during the day with little luck. In Morey's mind, a clock was ticking. His thought was that if they didn't make contact with the enemy, he would have to submit a negative report, and that might result in the teams being pulled off the job. He thought over everything they had done to try to determine if they had missed any opportunities. He understood that the contractors weren't as good at patrolling as the military. They were men who felt vulnerable in the open and when presenting themselves as targets, but he thought they had done a good job. He had split his team up with him in the lead with Drew and Rapp and with the others fanned out behind them. He felt confident that with Drew and Rapp, he would ferret out threats and would engage them forcibly.

As they moved along in the fading day, there was little conversation because the contractors, being armed for work, had all fallen into character. They wore baseball caps backward, pressed under headgear, and earphones that allowed them to communicate with all members of the team. Each man wore sunglasses that reflected the open land ahead, and all had their fancy weapons swiveling back and forth, engaging imaginary targets.

Kuk was a small village on the top of a broad mesa on which poppy fields stretched into the distance. There were vehicles, but most of the work was done by hand. People could be seen stooped among the rows of flowers. In another time and place, it would have been a landscape scene for an artist, but in Afghanistan it boded death.

The contractors bypassed what they thought was the hub of activity, searching for the war they wanted to come to them.

Morey stewed. "Shit, this might have been a mistake. I don't think we are going to find a fight here."

"Corporate isn't going to like it," Charlie Drew said, stating the obvious.

"Why don't we reposition to the edge of town to see if we can find a fight?" Bill Rapp was looking for a solution to their problem. "As the day comes to an end, people will be moving around. Maybe then we'll spot something."

Repositioning didn't help the contractors because any Afghans seen seemed to disappear as soon as the Americans appeared. Morey and his two partners couldn't get close enough to anyone to be considered a threat. Being out of their trucks and feeling the stress of having to concentrate on their every step weighed on them physically and mentally. They were more comfortable driving and presenting a threatening appearance from vehicles. The stress of having to think about their every movement shortened tempers. There was a lot of griping, but they pushed forward.

All the contractors wore big watches, but they didn't need them. The sun arcing across the sky told them that daylight was running out. They didn't want to be away from their compound at night. It was the sense of wasting another day without results that played on their minds, but it bothered Morey the most. He was the one who was going to have to report the day's failure to corporate. He was angry at himself, at his team, and mostly at the Afghans for not coming out of hiding and putting up a fight. With wild thoughts swirling in his head, he focused on the Afghans; they were the reason he was failing.

It happened quickly. Two boys, maybe seven years old, ran into the trail ahead of Bill Rapp, chasing a soccer ball. Not expecting to see the Americans, they froze. Rapp felt insulted that the boys had gotten in his way and thought he'd display American superiority and scare the boys by shooting up their soccer ball. He didn't aim carefully. His shots got close to the ball. The shooting triggered the pent-up emotion in Charlie Drew and Dave Morey, who were unaware that Rapp was trying to destroy the ball. In their minds, the boys became a threat. They fired at them. People who hadn't been seen all day emerged to try to save the boy, but their movement was perceived as a threat. The three men, who were away from others on the team, slaughtered anyone who moved in a frenzy of bloodlust. Determining the hut the people had emerged from, they attacked a low adobe wall and killed anything that moved behind it.

When the other groups caught up with Morey and his team, someone yelled, "Cease fire!" Even with that, the frenzied firing continued.

"Jesus Christ. What the fuck are you doing?"

The words got through to the shooters.

"You killed a bunch of civilians." Several of the joining team went over to inspect the bodies. "No weapons. It looks like a family." The words took the edge off the shooters.

"This is fucked up. And we're a long way from our compound. We'd better get in our trucks and beat feet before word of this gets out and the road behind us is closed."

All the contractors knew that was good advice. While the opium traders had satellite phones, the opium telegraph, word of mouth, had an uncanny way of rivaling modern communications for speed of dissemination.

"Wait," Morey ordered. "Search the hut for weapons. We have to find something to give us a cover story."

The team knew that it was good advice. Four men entered a sun-dried brick structure. After several minutes, one emerged with a weapon that looked like an old flintlock rifle, a relic from the wars the Afghans fought against the British a hundred years prior.

"This is it." The contractor carrying the weapon showed the others.

"There has to be more." Morey could foresee that if the slaughter was predicated on an old flintlock, the cover story he was conjuring wouldn't hold up to scrutiny.

"This is it. We turned over everything in the hut, and this is it," argued the contractor holding the weapon.

"I've got a couple of AK-47s back in Kabul," Charlie Drew mentioned. "When we get back there, we can switch them out for this piece of shit. That should make everyone happy."

"Let's figure out our story back at the compound. It wouldn't be a good idea to be traveling back in the dark," someone offered.

The team loaded into the trucks. A want to escape what would become a dangerous place occupied everyone's mind. Little thought was given to the human carnage left behind.

Once they felt safe, the gravity of what had been done began to sink into the contractors in every truck, but none more than the truck containing Morey, Drew, and Rapp. They were the gunmen. They had started working on a cover story.

"Who fired the first shots?" Morey asked.

"I guess I did." Rapp was embarrassed.

"What did you see? Were there people with guns?" Morey was asking the questions he knew his bosses would ask him.

"I was just trying to have some fun. I was trying to shoot up the soccer ball."

"Jesus, why didn't you tell us?" Drew realized that a lot of people had been killed because his partner hadn't told him and Morey what he was doing. Thinking they might be under attack, they had fired on anything that moved.

"I can't report that to corporate. Let's think about this. The two boys approached us, and it looked as if one might have had an explosive vest on. When we told them to stop, they rushed at us and we took them under fire. That's when we were attacked by people who were lying in wait. Something like that might fly, but if you have any ideas, let me know, because I'm going to have to report this as soon as we get back to the compound."

"That might be a tough sell." Drew the former policeman demurred. "The kids were pretty young, and they were wearing T-shirts that pretty much outlined their bodies. You could see they weren't belted."

"No one is going to know that but us," Morey cut off the argument. "And no one is going to find out about it, because once we decide on our story, that is going to be the only one put out."

"How about the rest of the team? They might have been close enough to have seen what happened," Drew said.

"We are going to put out one story line. If anyone was close enough to observe what happened, they won't say a word, because what we did today is going to be sold as what we came to do. If anyone complains, they'll lose the bonus money—and I don't see that happening. So, let's get our story straight so that we and sell it to the others and sell it to corporate as mission accomplished."

"Sounds good," Rapp agreed.

"Let's put the details together so that under any questioning no one goes off on a tangent." Morey knew that with the pretense for the air war in place, no one was going to look too closely at what happened. "Since you were the first shooter, Bill, tell us what you saw and how you reacted."

Rapp, understanding he was part of a play in which he was both the playwright and the principal actor, wanted to make sure his lines were clear. "Out of the corner of my eye, I saw movement in the trees along the trail that we were following. It was suspicious. At about that time, two boys started running at us. It looked like one of the boys had a bulky apparatus strapped to him. I told him to stop and fired a warning shot, but both boys continued at us. When I felt we were in danger, I fired one more warning shot, to no avail. When the boys were close enough so that if they exploded the vest, we would have been in the frag pattern, you guys fired with the intent of stopping them. With the threat disposed of, people who were waiting in ambush exposed themselves, and the three of us took them under fire." Rapp stopped. "Do you think that will pass muster?" he asked.

"I think that covers everything," Morey affirmed. "Now, when the entire group gets together, that's the story we'll sell. I don't think anyone was close enough to us to contradict us."

"What about the fact that we didn't find any weapons on any of the bodies?" Drew wanted all the story lines jibing.

"We didn't know the people were unarmed. And that's not important anyway. They were in the process of attacking us. When we get back to Kabul, we'll present the AKs you said you have as evidence the people were armed." Morey had his story set to report to higher headquarters.

Bivens drove to the marine encampment. He was looking haggard, which was nothing new for him. When he traveled alone, he refrained from wearing cameras strung from his neck and tried to blend in with the locals by wearing articles of Afghan clothing. He was especially careful not to draw attention to himself with Xyze personnel looking for him. Following his instincts, he assumed that since Xyze had failed in Bada the previous day, they would go farther out looking for their war. Knowing that Xyze would only go to places that were accessible by road, he thought about the villages they might enter. He guessed Kuk because it was known for its hardcore fighters. No one was sure whether the fighters were Taliban or drug traffickers, but whatever the case may be, it was a place better left alone. Sensing the contractors would go to a village where they might stir up a fight, he left in darkness, dressed as an Afghan, and drove there.

While he was looking for a story, he wasn't looking to be captured by Xyze. so he stayed in the home of the local constable arranged for by Aziz. There, he knew any events from the outlying area would filter through, so he could get his story.

Having been out all night, he arrived in the early morning as the marines were awakening and starting their daily routine. He didn't stop to talk with anyone but made his way to a fire where water was heating so that the marines could make their MRE coffee. He was always an amusement to the Americans. Whereas they poured their powdered coffee into the hot water in their canteen cups and drank it down quickly, Bivens had a ritual. He carried loose tea in a plastic bag. He individually plucked leaves from the bag and laid them in hot water as if he were in the process of making a witches' brew. While most of the marines were on the second and third cups of coffee, Bivens waited for his tea to take on the proper color, indicating it was ready to be consumed. During the entire brewing process, he didn't speak. He savored the aroma of the tea, which, after being carried around Afghanistan in a plastic bag, had lost most of its scent.

"I was told you were back in camp." Santiago approached him.

"I'm glad you're awake because I need a favor." Bivens smiled.

"Sure. What can the Marine Corps do for you?"

"I think I'm going to be in big trouble, and I'm going to have to lie low for a while. I was wondering if there was someway to hide my truck and more importantly hide me until Xyze determines they won't be able to snuff out the story I spent most of the night writing. I uplinked it an hour ago."

"That bad, huh?"

"Yes. I would have run it by you before filing it, but I felt it was too time-sensitive. I felt that if it didn't get out quickly, the war machine would be alerted, and then there would be hell to pay." Bivens was enjoying stringing the sergeant major along.

"Are you going to tell me about it, or do I have to guess?"

"Not in your wildest imagination could you guess this."

"I'm pretty cynical."

"Not nearly enough for this."

"Now you've got me curious. How about telling me what's going on?"

"We both know that Xyze was sent here to find a pretext that could be used to unleash the dogs of war. Well, they did."

"Oh, fuck." Santiago wasn't thinking about what Xyze had done but about the war that was about to begin. "This isn't good."

"That's exactly what I thought, and that is why I got my story off as quickly as possible. I felt that by exposing what had happened, any pretext for war would be eradicated. I wanted the information in the US press before people could pound their chests and call for war."

"Tell me what you wrote."

"There was a massacre in Kuk. Nineteen people were killed. I don't know what Xyze's cover story is going to be, but I was with the constable—he equates to your sheriffs—inspecting the aftermath. Two young boys were killed. There was a girl, maybe two, who was also killed, along with six men who were considered grandfathers, old men crippled from other wars or overwork. The rest were women of various ages. After a thorough search of the hut and area around where they were killed, the constable found no weapons. Nor were any explosives found. Witnesses reported that one souvenir was taken by the Americans: a weapon that had been used in the fight against the British and had been in the family for decades. No one was sure if the weapon had been fired in a hundred years. It was a relic, a symbol of family pride. As witnesses tell it, there was a family gathering to celebrate the pregnancy of one of the girls. The celebration was being held behind the home's wall, so it wasn't detectable from the path where the Americans walked. Young boys, as they do anywhere in the world, were playing with a ball that somehow got out of the confines of the walls. Naturally, they chased it, only to surprise Xyze, who were there looking for a fight. Xyze shot and killed the boys, and once the elders realized what was happening, they showed themselves to protest. The constable assumes that the boys approached the contractors. It is unclear whether they were warned off, but it wouldn't have done any good with one boy. He was a product of the war. His head was scrambled, so his brother had to guide him. He was a kid who wouldn't know danger. Anyway, both boys were killed, and then the extended family became the target. From the reports the constable received, the contractors attacked the wall and killed everyone behind it. I was with the constable when he conducted his search. It was a bloodbath. While the village started its grieving, I realized that the events could be reformatted and spun into a story that would serve as a cause for war. I thought if that were attempted, there would be lives wasted on a lie. And having witnessed the carnage up close, I couldn't let that happen to the population of the valley. Not if I could help it. That's why I uplinked the story without giving you a quick read."

"Jesus, nineteen civilians." Santiago was thinking about what he was going to have to do. "We have to get out of Afghanistan. The longer we spend here, the more our moral fiber is eroded. Instead of progressing as humans, we seem to be reverting."

"I just gave you the highlights of the story. In the piece that I filed, I went into detail, citing all the gory facts that the constable put together. It isn't a pretty piece, but if it hits the US media, it is going to give your people pause before they pull the trigger."

"Nigel, you may have done the world a favor. I hope so." Thinking of his immediate problems, Santiago asked, "Do you suppose that Aziz is aware of what happened?"

"Of course. Nothing goes on that he doesn't know about."

"That's what I figured. So you might want to rethink staying here for protection. Aziz might decide to wipe this camp out."

"Don't be too quick to judge what he might do. Obviously, he'll have to do something to show his people that he is in control, but he still wants to avoid an air war, so he might not attack. He might seek retribution in a different form," the Englishman spoke candidly.

"Any ideas on what he might want?"

"I haven't a clue, but I don't think it will be too long before he makes his wishes known."

"Yeah." Santiago shook his head in disgust. "What in the hell could Xyze have been thinking? They just beat one rap for killing civilians, and now this. I hope your story blows the lid off these guys. They are more trouble than they're worth. All they do is go around making messes that eighteen- and nineteen-year-old soldiers and marines have to clean up. They make the big money, and kids bleed for their mistakes."

"That's what the United States bought into when they decided to field mercenaries, but it has been that way throughout history. People who go to war for money are troublesome because they can't be relied on. Their allegiance is to cash, and as paymasters change, so do loyalties."

———

Abby Dunne had taken on the role as Stanley Weeks's most relied-upon assistant, and as such she showed up at the office early every morning to ensure her boss had the information from around the world. She liked the quiet time before the bulk of the staff arrived, using it to think about her day and how she would approach the problems that she expected to arise, knowing there would be a crisis that would have to be addressed that would throw off her schedule. As Baron had outlawed the *Washington Post* in federal offices, she had picked up her copy at home and carried it to work to read during the quiet time. Taking the paper out of a plastic bag designed to keep it dry on a rainy morning, she glanced at the lead story. It dealt with government corruption, hardly worth reading. Government corruption could have been the lead story every day. Moving through the headlines, her heart stopped. There was a report of a massacre in Afghanistan in which contractors had killed nineteen unarmed people. In reading the article, she was horrified, not that the massacre had occurred, but that it might slow down implementing the air battle that was supposed to end the war. The descriptions of the deaths were gory. The name of the company whose contractors were alleged to have committed the crime was brought out in the story.

The first thought that ran through her mind was what effect this isolated event would have on the plan. Would it change anything? She then thought of the more near-term problems that she would face. It was at Baron's request that contractors had been introduced into the Zukan Valley. Abby didn't know how that was going to play out in the NSC staff meeting. One thing she was sure of was that the president would distance himself from the fact, and that meant someone, most likely someone on the NSC staff, would take the blame. Since she was the lead planner, she started thinking of ways in which to cover herself.

Knowing the president wouldn't read the newspaper and Fox News wouldn't run a story that might be critical of his administration, she called her boss, who hadn't yet left for the office.

He was sipping his coffee when his cell phone buzzed. He looked at the caller ID. Seeing it was Dunne, he knew the call must be important because he'd told his staff he didn't want to be bothered at home for anything other than a national emergency.

"Weeks here." He made his irritation known by his tone.

"Sir, this is Abby. I hate to bother you, but I'm going to need your guidance." Her voice had a tinge of panic to it.

"Yes, what is it?"

"Have you read the *Washington Post* this morning or looked at any of the cable news channels?" She added the latter because the story was circulating through all media.

"No. You know I don't read the news rags."

"In that case, I'll paraphrase what is being reported." She described the events, giving her boss an idea of what he would be facing when he got into the office.

"That's not good." Weeks had stated the obvious. "Listen, it should take me a half hour to get there. Find out what you can from the White House staff without raising this to the presidential level. We'll figure out how we want to handle it." He hung up and moved more quickly than was his preference, knowing that he was facing a crisis.

By the time Weeks reached his office, the staff was abuzz with people trying to get some read on how the story was playing at the White House. No one seemed to care that a massacre had taken place, other than in the ways it might trigger the president. While taking Xyze's interpretation of the events, which was starting to filter out, and trying to determine if it rose to the level of an event that would allow the real war to start, the news stories painted an awful picture.

Weeks waited until midmorning before calling Baron. "Good morning, sir," he said in his cheeriest voice. "Have you had a chance to be briefed on the latest events out of Afghanistan?"

"Sort of. I got a call from Erik King, who told me his boys had given us the opening we've been looking for to start the air war." The president was happy. He could see the end of the Afghan commitment.

"Did Mr. King explain to you what the pretext for war was?"

"He didn't get into the details, but he said his people did what the military couldn't, so we have our opening. I intend to make a speech from the Oval Office this afternoon telling the country that the Afghans attacked us and we are going to seek retribution. Retribution plays well with my religious followers."

"I know you don't watch any channels other than Fox, but they aren't covering the story. Take a look at CNN." Weeks gave the president time to switch channels.

"Goddamn lame-stream media. They have it wrong. Erik told me there was an attack on his people."

"That's not what the reporter who was on the scene says. I am told that he has photos of the massacre site and that they have already reached Al Jazeera. That means they will be hitting our media soon."

"Is the reporter the same guy who has been making what we are trying to do look bad?"

"Yes, sir, it is."

"I thought we were going to take care of him. Why is he still walking around? Get rid of him." The words came in rapid-fire succession.

"Sir, you assigned that task to Mr. King. Xyze was supposed to handle it."

"Goddamn, can't anyone do anything right? Where does this leave us?"

"We have to play down the idea that a massacre took place. I've got my best people developing a counternarrative to knock down the most flagrant details of the story. That's normal Washington work. What I need is your guidance on what our next steps should be." Weeks didn't want to make the decision because he knew that if anything were to go wrong, he was going to be the fall guy.

"That's why I have an NSC. You guys are supposed to give me options."

Weeks was stuck because the consensus of his staff was that using the massacre as a pretext for war was a losing proposition. The world wouldn't buy furthering the war on a blatant lie with the United States compounding its error on the back of an atrocity. "Mr. President, I have called around to other agencies, and the consensus seems to be that the air war should be put off."

After a long pause, the president said, "Don't do anything. I'm going to call around to some people. We'll decide what to do later."

With their work done, Morey's team spent the night tightening up their story. Xyze was reporting that the team had been under heavy attack and it was only through their skills that they had escaped unscathed. Their narrative was bought by corporate because it made everyone look good. Morey knew there was one more step that had to be accomplished before everything reported could be wrapped in a tight package. He promised he would turn over the captured weapons when his team returned to Kabul. With corporate buying into his account of events, all that remained to be done was to ensure that Charlie Drew could get his hands on the AKs quickly once the team arrived in Kabul.

With corporate buy-in, a helicopter was scheduled to arrive the following evening to extract the team from the Zukan Valley. They couldn't get an exact time for their pickup, but they were assured the air war wouldn't start until after they were gone. Escape plans were made with no idea that Bivens's story was rattling around Washington. As ignorance is bliss, the team enjoyed their last day in the Zukan, drinking and thinking about how they were going to spend their bonus money.

Two contractors were assigned to provide watch on the exterior of the building where the festivities were taking place. These two men, able to hear the revelry, felt dejected at having been excluded from it. Their thoughts were with their coworkers at the party, so they didn't notice what was happening around the compound. Every Afghan had vanished as if an eraser had been rubbed over them. When the guards were relieved by drunken cohorts, they didn't report anything unusual because they hadn't noticed anything.

It wasn't until midafternoon that the first breaths of concern arose.

One of the guards reported to Morey that something strange was happening. The area around the compound was deathly still, void of human activity. Even the fields in the distance, which usually had workers in them, were empty. Except for the Americans, the compound and its surrounding area was a ghost town and eerily silent.

Morey woke several of the contractors and had them explore the structures within the walls where Afghans had remained housed, but they found every building empty. The island of life was the Americans.

Calling the group together, Morey detected that the exuberance of the previous evening had faded and was now replaced with concern. The contractors understood that they had become easily defined targets. They had heard Morey's boast to the marine sergeant major that he was an ex–artillery officer who understood the trajectories of overhead fire. They had bought that explanation while there were

Afghans near so that no one would fire on them, but there were no longer any Afghans. They could only hope Morey knew what he was talking about.

"This isn't good," Morey stated the obvious. "Get you gear ready to travel. I'm going to call and get the helicopter in here ASAP."

The call was placed, and to the team's chagrin, their extraction was not a priority. They would have to wait hours before a helicopter arrived.

Morey faced a difficult situation. He could have requested an immediate pickup by declaring an emergency, but to do so would have indicated he was in imminent danger. But since no shots had been fired, his request would be questioned. There was nothing more embarrassing than to have a contracting team declare an emergency when one didn't exist except in the minds of a team feeling mental pressure. To be picked up without shots being fired would be a humiliation that he didn't want to face. The competition between teams for bonus jobs was brutal. If he were to run away from a fight before the fight started, then other teams would use it to ridicule him, the result being that he wouldn't be used again. He bit his tongue and decided to wait for the scheduled extraction. It was a nervous time, made more nerve-racking by the calls the Morey team was receiving from higher-ups wanting additional details about the incident. Somewhere in the calls, the word *massacre* was mentioned, which sent chills throughout the team. After repeated contacts, the questions became more pointed, contradicting the report that had been filed.

The story of what had happened had gotten out. Morey realized when he arrived in Kabul he might have to report the events as they had occurred. With time, he could refine his story into something that he could sell, but with so much on his mind, he was having difficulty cobbling a salable story together. Understanding that there were people in Washington who would buy into any fabrication because it provided a pretext to commence the air war, he had to worry about those who would seek to get to the bottom of what was openly being referred to in communications as a massacre. They would be looking to assign blame. He knew if that happened, he would be in jeopardy. His idea was that in preventing a stain to the corporate image, Xyze would cover him, realizing that neither ISSAC nor Xyze would ever let a story out that indicated one of their teams had been involved in a war crime.

The wait for the helicopter gave each team member a chance to reflect on what they were involved with. Instinctively, they sensed that it was something that wasn't going to go away. Each man thought about his part in what had occurred. Hard questions would come, but in their minds, most of the team rationalized they had done nothing wrong other than being at the wrong place at the wrong time. Most hadn't been near the shooting and were accessories to it just for being part of the team. Those who hadn't fired distanced themselves from those who had.

The wait for the pickup helicopter dragged on. The stillness of the compound was palpable. Nothing moved, and that played on the minds of those waiting to escape. As the hour of pickup neared, there was hope. Finally, they would get to the safety of Kabul, where Morey could sculpt a story into something the company would buy and pass onto Washington.

The sun was setting, lighting the sand-infused air with a yellow glow. The helipad to be used for the pickup was outside the walls of the compound and only a short walk away, but the distance seemed formidable. For safety, the team wouldn't leave the compound walls until the helo landed. Then they would dash to it, leaving most of their gear behind.

The pickup chopper wasn't a military aircraft. It was owned by Xyze and was being used because no emergency had been reported and the landing zone was considered benign. It was an easy run. Plus, by not using the military, Xyze could charge for the service.

Radio contact was made with the helo. A sigh of relief swept through the team as they could hear the craft approaching. With the rotor noise distinguishable, the team moved from behind the compound walls and, with weapons at the ready, ran for their pickup.

The helo was in its final approach, when a mortar round exploded the dirt patch in which it was supposed to land.

"Abort, abort" were the words the team heard over their radio. The helo pulled up and banked sharply. "Team leader, the zone is hot. We can't land in a hot zone," one of the pilots explained. "We've gotta get out of here." In a minute more, the helo had disappeared. Morey and his team were confused. The confusion lasted until the ground, which had minutes before had seemed sterile and devoid of life, came alive. Shots were fired at the team, forcing them back behind the compound walls.

Sergeant Major Jaio Santiago had received Bivens's report, but as bits of information came to him, they amplified the story. Santiago had help in deciphering the clues. Bivens provided the names of the three shooters. Santiago knew Morey but not the other two. With the details of what had happened, he tried to figure out what was about to happen to the marines.

"You know, the way this unfolding is odd. It's almost as if Aziz has something planned and is going to exact revenge." Bivens was airing his thoughts.

"What do you mean?" Santiago was thinking along similar lines but wanted to hear to Englishman's thoughts as confirmation.

"You were the one who told me the Taliban have their mortars preregistered on every target in the valley."

"They do."

"And they showed that by putting two rounds dead center on the landing pad." Bivens hesitated. "If they have that capability, why not fire when the helo landed and destroy it? Even more puzzling is that if they have the capability to destroy the Xyze compound, why hasn't it been done? If Aziz wanted quick revenge, he could have had the compound and its occupants obliterated. But that hasn't happened. Why?"

The sergeant major hadn't thought along those lines, but he agreed with what he was hearing. "You wrote the story about Xyze being sent here to gin up a cause for a wider war. If Aziz wipes them out, the story of the massacre will vanish. Then the killing of the contractors will do just what they were sent here to do, provide an excuse for the air war to begin."

As the thought hadn't occurred to him, Bivens mulled it over. "I think you're right, but that doesn't diminish the fact that he can't let the contractors go free. In order to save face among his people, he will have to exact some form of revenge. The massacre is too big an event to be swept away. We know that he has the ability to destroy the compound and its inhabitants, but so far hasn't done it. Is it to prevent a wider war in which this valley would be destroyed? He's playing a game, and I have no idea what that game might be."

"Somewhere in the middle must lie the answer. When he is ready to act, I'm sure we'll have front-row seats." Santiago didn't know what else to say.

They didn't have long to wait for an answer. Trucks that delivered the marines root vegetables arrived at the camp for their morning delivery. It looked like part of the daily routine where marines would off-load the two trucks, hoping they would be provided with vegetables that they could chop up and put in their MREs. A change in diet was important to the young men, but not important enough that they would let the trucks into their camp. Even though they knew the drivers and had a good relationship with them, they locked them out so that no explosives would enter the area where the marines lived.

Santiago and Bivens watched the off-loading and noticed something different.

"Something is fucked up," Santiago said as he started to move toward the trucks. Instead of only a driver in the trucks, the seats were occupied with people who were crammed in. A spike of fear ran through him. He intended to pull the marines back. As he approached, the doors of one truck opened and three men stepped out, showing deference to one in their midst. The man was in workmen's clothes like the others, but he didn't have their worn look. On seeing Santiago and Bivens, he removed his headgear and the scarf that kept the incessant grit in the air off his face.

Recognizing Aziz, Bivens said nonchalantly, "I guess we are going to find out what he has planned for the Xyze compound."

"Looks that way, but I'm not worried about that. I'd like to know what he has planned for us."

When Santiago greeted his guest, it was the first time that the marines discovered that their sergeant major could speak a language other than English.

The marine and the Englishman led the aristocrat to the camp stools where they had been sitting, noticing that he was reluctant to dirty himself. He did sit with them, but he seemed uncomfortable.

"Would you like a tea?" Bivens asked in Pashto.

"The Americans have spoiled me. I drink Colombian coffee. It was one of the things my CIA handlers thought I might like."

"I can get you a coffee, but it will be powdered coffee." Santiago was amused at how easily the finer things in life could become habit-forming.

Aziz, smiling at the suggestion of powdered coffee, refused.

"I came here as a peasant because the situation on the ground has changed. After the US contractors murdered my people, a CIA handler contacted me. I suppose he thought that with the killings, I would strike out at the murderers and provide reason to start the air war. He asked what I intended to do, hoping I would tell him so that he could report back to his superiors. He said the air war was on hold because of the confusion over what happened in Kuk, and he cautioned me not to do anything that would surely start the war. He made it sound as if I am now the person who has the ability to save this valley."

"I hadn't thought of that," Bivens spoke, "but it's typical American thinking: blame the other guys for their mistakes."

"Since we are on the eve of war, I assume I am a target now. That is why I chose to come here in disguise. With my reputation for elegance, I thought your drones would overlook the vegetable delivery. I suppose the ruse worked, because I am here."

"Did your handler offer you a deal?" Bivens asked.

"I have had the Americans catering to me for almost forty years. I can't remember a day when they haven't been near, as if I were their most prized possession. When many of them disappeared silently in the night, I understood I may be in trouble. It was you, Sergeant Major, who told me that the CIA might not be briefed on the war plans. That made sense for a while. But by running away, they somehow learned of those plans."

"Sounds that way." Santiago was terse.

"Since I have the marines trapped in this location, I may have to use you as bargaining chips to forestall the air war." Aziz merely stated it as fact.

"In a sane world, it might work out that way, but you are basing your assumptions on the idea that the marines are important in all this. We are a small marine unit commanded by sergeants. We could be written off in the narrative of what is going to happen. I'm sure there are people in Washington right now writing about our bravery in fighting off your hordes."

Aziz smiled. He had been around the Americans enough to know they could polish a turd and sell it.

"There must be some way to forestall this thing." Santiago was concerned about the loss of life that would take place on both sides.

"I thought that by sparing the mercenaries' compound, I might use them to change the minds of the war makers."

"Is that why you scared the helicopter away?" Bivens had more curiosity about the event than did Santiago, who was still thinking about the words expressing that the marines were in peril.

"Yes."

"To what end?" Bivens persisted.

"Our representatives who have been in contact with the Americans during the negotiation process advised that I make a grand bargain for the contractors. They mentioned that your story hasn't fed fully into the news, but it has gained enough attention so that questions are now being asked. Their suggestion was that the war won't start until the contractors are safe, so it behooves me to keep them alive. What they overlook is the fact that in order to continue to lead my people, I have to exact some revenge for these murders. That is the puzzle."

"Why not separate the problems?" Bivens was racing out ahead of the others. "Only three of the contractors were the killers. Why not exact your revenge on them and make a grand gesture by freeing the others? You could turn them over to the marines. That might buy you some time. If my story gets into the forefront of the US media, even the Americans will recognize that what these men did was evil. In fact, I'll start writing a follow-up story that will blow the lid off this entire charade."

"There is a hole in your reasoning." Santiago mulled over what he was hearing. "The US status of forces agreement requires that all personnel charged with crimes in Afghanistan be returned to the United States to stand trial."

Bivens was ready with an answer. "These men haven't been charged with crimes, and they aren't military covered by status of forces. With that loophole, before US justice becomes involved, there seems to be an exception period." Bivens smiled at his convoluted logic, knowing lawyers would shred his argument.

Santiago wasn't convinced. "It a nice theory, but it won't fly."

"It will if the problem goes away before these men are charged with any crime."

Aziz spoke, "If I destroy the contractors, their crime will go unnoticed in what I fear will be the destruction of the valley. I could exact revenge to please my people, but then I would have to watch as they were destroyed." He paused. "You two know Western ways.

That is why I came to you looking for an answer that might appease the Americans and get them to hold off the war."

"Nigel's story of the massacre is beginning to bubble up in the US news media. If that story grows, the people in Washington who want this war will be unable to act." Santiago had added what he thought might be a solution to the problem.

"If it doesn't happen quickly, it will be too late. I fear the Americans' thirst for a wartime accomplishment far outruns the pace of the media. The story of the massacre will become a footnote to the glamour of the war," Aziz spoke, while thinking of finding a way out of his dilemma.

"I see this as a two-sided problem." Nigel, always the conniver, smiled as he spoke. "You need to exact revenge," he said to Aziz, "while trying to forestall a war that won't do anyone any good." The Afghan nodded in agreement. "There are two time lines that have to be considered to solve these problems. Obviously, the US war machine is preparing to commence the war. We don't know the timing, but we can surmise the gears are turning now. The second time line has to do with the Americans acknowledging the massacre took place and throwing their blanket of protection over the murderers. That will take a little more time. I feel it is the second time line that we have to beat, before blanket immunity can be given to the contractors. In that time, you have to exact your revenge." He again spoke at Aziz, "Because if you don't, you will lose your people before the air war starts."

"Are you telling me to destroy their compound?"

"Yes." Nigel was sure.

The sergeant major had no solutions, but he couldn't sit, knowing the moment the first mortars dropped, the marines were as doomed as the contractors.

"We are on the doorstep of war, a war looking for an excuse to start. If the contractors are killed, it will wipe out the gravity of what they did and will make them martyrs. That will be a sure cause for war. I'm saying this because once this thing starts, no one has any idea where it is going to end. We do know that a lot of people are going to die. The only bargaining chip you will have are the marines. You will have to use them, and then a bunch of kids who had their tickets punched to go home will be wasted."

Aziz nodded in agreement.

"Why not change the calculus? As far as we know, only three contractors were the killers. The others were in the vicinity and had no part in the shootings. Why not make a grand gesture that would play well in the media and with your people? Free those who were not accused of wrongdoing." Switching his attention to Bivens, the sergeant major asked, "Could you write a story that would make the magistrate look like a reasonable man, a person who could be negotiated with?"

"That's what I do for a living," the Englishman joked. "I could do it, but I'm trying to figure out where you're going with this."

"The magistrate has to exact revenge to keep his standing in the eyes of his people, but there is also a need for him to look like a reasonable man in the eyes of the West. He has a good reputation from working with the CIA, so a grand gesture would bring many defenders to his side. By exacting revenge on only the shooters and freeing the others, he can accomplish both." Turning his attention to Aziz, he asked, "Do you think that if you took the three shooters alive, you could keep them alive while they awaited an Afghan trial?"

The Afghan nodded, unsure of what he might be getting himself into. Before passing final judgment, he wanted to hear all the marine had to say. "Tell me your thoughts on this."

"With the three shooters alive at hidden locations throughout the valley, that would cause a delay in the bombings that have been planned. By keeping men who should die alive, you would have something to bargain with as Washington tries to bury the massacre. I feel the massacre won't sell well with the US public, and given the fact that you were reasonable in keeping alive those who were responsible for the massacre to await justice, you can forestall the air war. There will be efforts made to recover the contractors. I'm sure the CIA will show up at your door looking for your help. By keeping the murderers alive, I feel, you can stop the craziness. It would also give you cover with your own people who want revenge."

After a long period of reflection, Aziz nodded in agreement. "What you say solves a lot of problems, but you haven't mentioned the marines."

"No one cares what happens to them. They volunteered to serve their country for out-of-fashion ideas such as duty and honor. This far into the war, only money talks. I feel efforts will be made to save the contractors, and the marines will be a forgotten piece in this puzzle. I say that knowing that if we can't buy time in holding off the air war, the marines will be casualties. We're the price my country is willing to pay to salve their conscience enough to allow them to rationalize the wanton killings the air war will bring. What I'm suggesting is that we can buy time enough to get the marines out of the valley under the guise that we were the ones who saved the contractors. The American people would never buy extracting the contractors and leaving the marines behind to be killed. Can you write that story, Nigel?"

"I can write it so that it will bring tears to your eyes." The Englishman grinned. "I had no idea that you were so devious, Sergeant Major. But tell me, how do you intend to separate the contractors so that only the shooters remain?"

"I'm going to offer them a deal they can't refuse. I don't know what that deal is yet, but given how contractors work and given their affinity for money, there has to be a way.

<hr />

Aziz gave the sergeant major only the rest of the day to extract the nine contractors, if he could. After that, the compound would be attacked and destroyed. If the shooters gave up, Aziz agreed to keep them alive as bargaining chips.

Six Hummers were loaded with marines. Santiago didn't want to go into the contractors' compound alone and risk becoming their hostage. He wanted a force with him so that if he failed in what he was attempting, he could get out.

Arriving in a cloud of dust, the marines were not surprised to find the outer walls of the compound unguarded. The contractors understood the futility of their position and were going to make their last stand from one building.

Upon seeing the marines, they exposed themselves, thinking that the marines had been ordered to rescue them, when in fact no such orders had been delivered. In Washington, Baron's staff tried to bury the story of the massacre under a Presidential Proclamation that was rolled out to divert the public's attention. To keep the pressure off themselves, the staff kept Baron in the dark, feeding him only positive spin around the low media play the story of the massacre was receiving. The only unfiltered information Baron received was skewed because it was from Erik King, who painted a rosy picture of the situation as he was loath to admit the people in his company had committed an atrocity. While keeping Baron's spirits lifted, King worked the phones with contacts in the military, trying to put together a recovery mission, but like most things in the Pentagon, that would take some time. Something was being planned that would involve the marines in the valley, but no orders had been issued. All that was accomplished in the back-and-forth conversations between Xyze and the military was that the air war would be put off until the contractors were clear.

Word of a recovery had been leaked to the contractors in the compound, so upon seeing the marines, they thought they had dodged a bullet. Their crime would go unpunished and they would go home without having to discuss the killings.

Morey exposed himself as if shackles had been removed. "We've been waiting for you. We didn't expect you for another day or two. I'm sure glad the recovery was moved up. My men are getting a little tense."

"I figured they would be," Santiago spoke as the entire team of contractors showed themselves. "But you're reading something into my being here that you may be confused about. This is not the recovery or whatever it is you're waiting for. I'm here on my own with the permission of the magistrate."

The words took time to register with the contractors. If the marines weren't there to rescue them, then what was their purpose?

"You mean Aziz let you come here?" Morey was confused.

"Yes."

"But why?"

"You can understand that he has a problem. He can't let you out of the valley alive. To do so would diminish his position in the eyes of his people. If he were to lose his stature, he would no longer be able to govern or whatever it is that he does."

"Why did he send you? Why didn't he just finish us off?" Morey crowed as if that were his preferred option, but Santiago noticed that the men standing around Morey weren't as sure that they wanted to die. Several shuffled nervously.

"Here's the deal." Santiago waited until he was sure he had everyone's attention. "Aziz believes that only three of you are guilty of the killings and that everyone else were bystanders." Santiago paused and let his lead-in sink into the minds of those listening. "He asked me to come here with his deal. The three responsible shooters are to hand themselves over. I'm clear to take the others with me back to Marine Camp."

Morey balked instantly and angrily. "We're a team. We don't split up for anything or anybody. You can tell that to the Afghan pooh-bah."

Santiago was nonchalant. "If that's what you decide. I'll pass that along, but you should know that when the sun goes down today, this place will be leveled and all of you in it will die. I told you once that mortars were preregistered on everything in the valley, and now you know how good the mortarmen are. They waited until the helo was almost in the zone and managed to scare it away without damaging it. That was a message sent to you. This place will be wiped out," Santiago said with finality. "What you probably didn't know is that there are about a hundred twenty Taliban ready to mop this compound up after the mortars have stopped. None of you will be alive at sunrise."

There was a visible break in the "all for one, one for all" attitude that Morey parroted.

"Let's talk this out, Dave. Some of us who were not near you when you were shooting up those people think you overreacted."

"No, we stick together."

"What the hell do I gain if we stay?" another voice rose. "I came here to make money and pay for my retirement home. I didn't come to go home in a body bag."

That sentiment took hold with those who had not been involved in the shooting.

"We stay together as a team." Morey directed men who had no loyalty to him or to corporate warfare. They had come for a cash payout. What Santiago was describing was something they hadn't signed up for. They didn't want to die for another team member's mistake. They were coworkers with no other bond but the job. When they signed on to serve in Afghanistan, none had conceived of the possibility of dying for Xyze. It was a job with risks for which they were well paid, but the risks had always been managed. The dirty work and dying had always been farmed out to the military. What was facing them was the unmanaged fog of warfare, in which they could easily die.

"Dave, I was close enough to you to see that you and Bill shot at the kids without reason, and Charlie got caught up in the frenzy. It was like you went berserk. The rest of us were a distance from you, and as far as I know, none of us, other than you three, fired a round. This is on you, man. I don't think we should all go down. Those of us who have a chance to get out should take it."

The response of the group was what Santiago had expected. These men had no loyalty to one another. When something came between them and their money, they splintered, every man looking out for himself.

"Okay, here's the deal Aziz is offering. He wants the three shooters alive, and he promises to keep you alive to serve as bargaining chips. The president, after this fiasco, realizes the plans for an air war are a nonstarter and has hinted that we're once again going to negotiate our way out of Afghanistan. Aziz thinks he might be able to use the three of you as a prisoner exchange to gain further concessions. That said, he might kill you before you set foot out of this place. It's a chance you'll have to take. If I were you, I'd take it, because you are of more value to him alive than dead."

"What happens to those who will go with you?" Morey was flailing for a counterargument.

"When the marines get rotated out of the valley, they go with us." Santiago stopped to let the contractors think about the possibilities. "I'm going to go back to my Hummer to give you time to talk among yourselves and decide what you want to do. I know this is a huge decision, so take some time, but not too much, because I intend to be out of here before sunset."

"Who gave you permission to effect this recovery? The word we're receiving is that it is days off." Morey was trying to blunt Santiago's reason for being there.

"You're right. A recovery is in the works, but you said it yourself: it is days off. Your lights go out at sunset unless you buy into what I'm selling. The recovery, if and when it comes, could be more fiction in this war. I'm telling you, tonight is your endgame."

"You've got no right to take this on. I'm going to report you to higher headquarters." Morey was fighting hard, not so much for his team, but for himself.

"Great. You report. I'm getting in a Humvee and getting out of here. All I can say is, it's been a pleasure working with you." The sergeant major turned to walk away.

"Wait," someone in the group spoke up. "Give us some time to talk this over."

"Okay," Santiago mentioned as if he were doing them a favor, knowing full well what the decision was going to be. "One further thing: Kabul got a head shrinker into my camp to debrief any of you who decide to leave with me about the massacre. Someone wants to get a head start on looking into the possibility of your suffering from PTSD, so if any of you are coming along with me, you are going to have to endure a shrink asking questions about the massacre."

Santiago walked back to the marines and found Bivens, who was dressed in marine fatigues, with his hair shaved into a high and tight haircut. It was the price he was willing to pay to get what he considered the scoop of the war. The marines had done their best to make him look like one of them, but there were challenges. He was overweight, so they'd had difficulty finding a set of utilities that would harness his girth. He was passable, not as a marine, but as Dr. Meridith, as an oversized name tag identified him. He had conceived of the scheme, wanting the firsthand story from those contractors who were willing to escape before they got to safety and had a chance to piece together a story line that could be sold to their bosses. Bivens wanted their stories told while their feelings were raw and unfiltered. "Any luck?" he asked the sergeant major.

"They're coming apart. I'm sure we'll get most of them, and when we do, you can have a one-on-one with each of them. Be sure you extract their stories before they can put a story together that can be sold to the US public. Once they get to their PR people, I'm sure a story will be spun that will make them look heroic."

"Are you sure I can pass the smell test? Some of these guys might see through this disguise."

"None of them know what you look like. They have pictures of you that don't look anything like you look now. And besides, I sold you off as a Kabul plant sent here to get into the psychology of the massacre. Their boss, Morey, might be the only one who might recognize you, but he won't be in on the interviews. Those whom you'll be speaking to will be so relieved to be getting out of the compound that they won't bother to notice. Just tone down your accent as much as possible, and we'll be all right."

"You probably didn't know I was educated in France and can effect a passable French accent to cover my English."

"Let's hear it."

Bivens spoke a few sentences. Santiago realized Bivens hadn't exaggerated his prowess at being able to cover his English.

"C'est bon," Santiago said, using his French. "You got the inflections and tones down perfect."

"Sergeant Major, what else are you hiding?"

"Nothing," he answered. "Now let's think about how we want the interviews conducted. We'll use the back seat of the Hummer that hasn't been stripped and still has its shell on. It will be hot inside, but that will make the contractors uncomfortable. Before the first of the contractors arrive, put that phony cast on your leg and lay the assumed damaged leg out, taking up the whole back seat. Leave your crutch in a place where it can be seen. We'll bring in the contractors one at a time and place them on the passenger seat in front of you so that they will have to turn to see you. It should be fairly dark when the doors are closed. You can start questioning them before they have a chance to get comfortable and think things through. I know you're not a Catholic, but I want the setup as close to a confessional as we can manage. I think it will help them spill their guts."

"I had no idea that you were religious." Bivens laughed.

"I'm not, but confession is one of the things that has stuck with me. It's a place to unburden oneself of sin. With any luck, you'll be able to extract a lot in their want for atonement." Santiago was satisfied with the setup. "Are you ready to get their stories, Doctor Meridith?"

"Call me 'Father.' I like the priest idea and the idea of confession."

The sergeant major had no idea what was being discussed among the contractors, but he was surprised at how quickly a decision was made. The nine nonshooters wanted out of the valley. They were going to leave and wouldn't look back. Also, they were happy to accommodate the odd requests of the doctor whom military headquarters had sent from Kabul to check out their mental state. In a one-on-one setting, they jammed into the covered Hummer with the doctor and blurted out their stories. Most matched, but there were nuances that Bivens hadn't thought of. He learned how much each was going to be paid if they in fact could create an event that would start the air war. That tidbit was going to be in the forefront of the story he was formulating. As he talked to the men who were escaping, he changed from seeing them as contractors trying to make some quick money to seeing them as killers for hire.

With their stories and the nine contractors in hand, the marines left the compound area. Bivens had gotten enough information to write the story he thought would further dampen the ardor for war. Santiago wasn't sure of what his play would be in the unfolding saga, but he felt he had done the best he could in rescuing people who were accessories to murder only by location. There had been no planning by the contractors to kill innocents. They were looking for an entrée to war, and kids, men, and women trying to eke out an existence got in the way. With the sun almost down, he realized the other part of the play would be acted out, and he discovered that despite talk of going down in a blaze of glory, the contractors who had been left behind had surrendered to the Aziz Taliban without a whimper. They were disarmed, and following advice Bivens had given Aziz, they were photographed to show that they were receiving humane treatment. The photographs coupled with the story was all Bivens could do. He just had to write it up and wait.

———

Unlike with the other articles he had written that had been funneled through Al Jazeera and brought to a skeptical world press, it seemed the world was waiting for the final chapter of this story—and it was circulated quickly. It didn't make the *Washington Post* above the front-page fold, but it appeared in one-inch bold letters just below the fold, in a position that was impossible to ignore. While government employees were banned from reading the *Washington Post* in their offices, most government workers received their paper at home. They read it with breakfast and drove to work with a sense of foreboding. They didn't know how the information outlined in the story would reach the president, but they knew it would. No one could predict the mood that this would put Baron in. Most suspected it wouldn't be good. They hid in their offices, awaiting an explosion.

The first people called by Baron were his political advisers. He wanted a media strategy that would deflect attention from the fact that he had knowledge that an air war was supposed to follow the *casus belli*, the fabricated ground battle. The most easily scapegoated governmental entity was the military, but he was cautioned from accusing them because it was the marines who had saved the nine not involved in the killings. Bivens had made them seem heroic, painting the picture that they'd had to fight their way into the compound to rescue the trapped men. The hyperbole used in describing the bravery of young men in uniform and their sergeant major was an obstacle that was in the way of the president's scapegoating them.

There had to be some way to place the blame on someone not in the White House. The president sent out his political team to find that person. He himself conducted his own backtracking. The first call he made was to Erik King.

"This is the president," he spoke angrily the second King was on the line. "What the fuck happened? You told me your guys were clean in all this, but it turns out the Taliban have three of your people who participated in a massacre that you assured me didn't happen. What are you doing, playing me for a sucker? You stuck me with a problem that is going to throw off the timing of getting out of Afghanistan. Don't bullshit me. What's going on from your end?"

"Mr. President, you have a right to be angry, but—"

"You're damn right I do. And I want you to fix the mess your people created for me."

"We are working on a solution now. We haven't finalized any plans, but essentially we think we can use the marines already in the Zukan Valley to effect the rescue of those left behind."

"That's a nonstarter. We're already in over our heads. I want out of Afghanistan. I'm not taking on another mission that will keep us there longer." Baron was adamant.

"We may have to take on a recovery. The three people left behind could be tortured and killed, and that wouldn't look good. The fake news would run with that story, probably hyping the idea that you left Americans behind to die."

"The public is going to be a lot more critical if I attempt a rescue and get a bunch of marines killed rescuing men who massacred bystanders. Your men are paid well and are supposed to know what the hell they are doing. I ought to cut all the Xyze contracts and get rid of you." The president provoked the CEO.

"Mr. President, don't get out ahead of yourself. Xyze provides a service."

"A service that is expensive," Baron fumed. "You were supposed to take over some of the tough jobs to relieve the pressure on the military, and all you've done is scoop the easy things. You really haven't gotten your hands dirty. You're bilking me and not doing what you said you were going to do." The president wanted to provoke King. "Tell me why I shouldn't dump your whole operation?"

"Mr. President, with all due respect, Xyze has provided services that don't appear on the books. I floated around the world pushing your agenda with despots that the American people would not like to hear about. I was your secret envoy, and in essence that was work that Xyze did for you." King knew he had the president. All his back-channel work was marginally legal. He had ambassadorial status and power without ever having gone before the Senate for confirmation.

"Are you blackmailing me?" Baron, surprisingly, was not angry. He came from the rough-and-tumble world where everything was done off the books.

"No, sir, but you can see that if some of my private work for you were to leak out, it might not look good. I know you don't want that."

"You son of a bitch." There was a long pause. "Xyze stays on as a contractor, but I want the mess you created boxed. I want all the loose ends tied together before any snooping reporter finds out anything more. Speaking of reporters, I thought you told me this reporter was going to be silenced. His name is on the latest story. Why didn't you get that done?"

"We were about to close him out when news broke that those accused of murder were taken hostage, but I'll promise you this: If the son of a bitch is still in Afghanistan, he won't be walking out."

"Erik, I put a lot of trust in you. Get this thing done and done right without fingerprints. Can you do that?"

"Yes, sir."

Baron ended the call, puzzled that even his most trusted associates seemed incapable of doing the tasks they had advertised they could do.

"Get me Stan Weeks on the phone," he instructed an assistant.

"Yes, sir." The president impatiently waited until the call was placed.

The call was connected. Unlike the way he handled King, who was outside the government, he was more demeaning with the people he had placed in positions of power in the government.

"I want you to get the negotiations with the Taliban back on track. That dumb idea you had about fighting a battle that would get us out of Afghanistan is a bust. All I have gotten for trying to implement your scheme is bad press, and it has to stop."

Weeks didn't bother to mention that it was the president who had called him into the Oval Office and planted the idea of a final battle. He remained quiet, allowing the president to escape responsibility.

"Here's what I want you to do," Baron ordered. "Kill all the plans that are pending about starting an air war. That was a dumb idea." The president spoke as if he had had no part in approving the plans. "Then get the marines the hell out of their forward position. They didn't accomplish a thing and could become overrun, which would present us with a bigger hostage problem. I don't care how you do it, but get them out. Once that is done, get together with the State Department and tell them to revive negotiations. I'm going to announce this afternoon that there have been breakthroughs in our back channels that look like they might allow us to cut a deal."

"I was unaware that we had people still negotiating," Weeks spoke, immediately knowing he had made a mistake.

"We haven't, but only those close to this thing know that. Get involved and get the negotiations on track. I want a media splash that will wipe out the stories that are circulating about some contractors murdering civilians. That's the other thing I want you to do: Debunk the massacre story and dig up some dirt on the reporter who posted the story. We have to paint him as fake news. I want all the details of the massacre tied up. The story doesn't make me look good."

"Mr. President, how do you want to handle the three contractors who were left behind? According to the fake reporting, they will be used as bargaining chips. Do you want me to tell State that they should be part of the negotiations?" Weeks wanted to tie the president to any action taken at the negotiating table. He didn't want to be told later that the whole thing was his idea.

"They are not to be part of the deal. I want a negotiation that will be quick and sellable. Give the Taliban what they want. All that I require is the ability to say we made a deal that is good for the United States. It may not be what the military wants, but as long as I come off looking like the peacemaker, we'll cut the deal."

"Even at the expense of the Afghan government?"

"Especially at the expense of the Afghan government. Those bastards have milked this country for too long now. We have given them everything they need to win the war three times over and they still can't get it done. It's time that they stood on their own."

"Are you telling me that the State Department can tell the negotiators to cut the Afghan government free?" Weeks didn't want any misunderstanding on that point.

"Yes." The president reflected on what he had just said. "You can further inform State and the negotiators that it is the optics around this that are the important thing. We have to come off looking strong regardless of the results. I don't care how our leaving Afghanistan plays around the world; it has to play well in the US market. So once you tell me we are negotiating again, I'll do an interview with Fox and let them run with the story we want to get out. If I give them a big enough head start, the other fake news outlets won't be able to catch up before the story is planted and takes hold."

"I think I know what you want. I'll get right on it." Weeks did give a second thought to the idea of abandoning an ally, considering it might not be morally correct. He was concerned with following the president's orders and getting the PR strategy in place.

Baron made calls to his friends to alert them that there had been a change in plans before he made the intergovernmental calls to alert all parties involved that there had been a change. He'd use that latter opportunity to picked their brains as to what they thought a good PR strategy might be. Several came up with ideas that would put Baron at the forefront of claiming victory, and he liked that. He smiled at the irony of what he was attempting to do. He was going to define a strategy for leaving a war, a war that had rambled on for nearly twenty years without a clear-cut strategy. He was not only the ultimate dealmaker; he was also the ultimate peacemaker whom history would look favorably upon.

The sergeant major was making plans to send out another patrol, when the company clerk came into his bunker.

"You might want to read this, Sergeant Major." The words indicated nothing, but the clerk couldn't restrain his smile. Santiago knew it was good news.

Santiago took the message and read it. "Son of a bitch." He shook his head in agreement with what he'd just read. "Go get Bivens and bring him here," he instructed the clerk.

When the Englishman entered, Santiago handed him the message.

"Well, you did it, Sergeant Major. You leashed the dogs of war."

"It wasn't me. It was the power of the pen, your pen, that saved countless lives. And I'm grateful for that. While it looks like I'm going to be able to get my troops and the contractors out, I'm worried about you. You're a marked man. As I see it, no one is going to let you live long enough to see England again."

"That's rather dramatic," Bivens joked. "This isn't the first place where I have been marked for extermination. It is becoming a habit of mine. I'll figure something out that will protect these rosy English cheeks."

"That may not be so easy. You don't seem to be having the same luck as your hero. You definitely don't have anything near the safety net that Churchill had."

"Nor the money or the connections," Bivens joked.

Santiago liked the Englishman and thought he owed him for depicting the events on the ground that had gotten US politicians to call off the execution of their senseless plan. Without Bivens, the marines would have remained in the valley, and once the bombs started falling, Santiago could see no way that he could have gotten all his men out alive, because the tenuous truce between him and Aziz was sure to shatter. And the battle to end the war would have caused marine deaths.

"I think I got what I wanted out of this, but I'm worried about you." The marine showed his affection for the newspaperman.

"You know, Sergeant Major, when we reporters take on these assignments in dangerous places, we know the risks. Of course, we think we might die in the heat of a battle. None of us think we'll be hunted down like dogs marked for extinction. It kind of demeans the profession." Bivens smiled, but his concern was evident in his tone.

"Where would you be safest?"

"I suppose in England. There hasn't been a reporter killed there in years."

"Is there any way you can get there?" Santiago was thinking. "Do you have any sources who might help you travel out of Afghanistan safely?"

"As you know, with my prickly personality and charm, I tend to burn bridges and piss people off. I can't think of anyone who would risk anything to help me. At times like this, it makes me feel that I should have been nicer to a whole lot of people." Bivens shook his head, knowing that he had lived his life and done things just the way he had wanted to. There was no going back. He had left a path of destruction wherever he set foot. "You know, Sergeant Major, it's a wonder I haven't pissed you off, but given time, I bet I could."

Santiago laughed. "There is no doubt about that."

"Tell you what. Let's do what Churchill would have done in a crisis like this and drain a bottle of brandy."

"We did that last night," the sergeant major informed him.

"Well, that was poor planning. What do you have to drink to my obituary?"

"I think I may be able to scrounge some bourbon from the troops."

"It's a comedown, but as friends, we ought to close out our friendship with a toast."

"I'll get the booze." Santiago left the bunker in search of something to celebrate with. He felt odd, as if he should do something for the Englishman. He didn't want to think that Bivens had given countless Afghans and his marines a chance to live at the expense of his own life.

Returning with a half-filled bottle of bourbon, Santiago placed in on the map table between them. "Before we get much deeper into this morbid play, let's think. If you were returning to England on personal leave, how would you do it?"

Bivens thought. "I suppose first I would have Aziz write me a letter of safe passage. Then I'd travel to Kabul. From there, I would take a flight to Qatar, where I'd check in with Al Jazeera and fly home." Bivens became nostalgic for the seeming ease of his former life. "With the number of people who will be looking for me, you can see I'm pretty much stuck here, having to wait out my hunters, because you know with the air war in suspension, Xyze will flood this area with their crackerjack teams, looking to take my scalp."

"You can see from Xyze's last performance that they have no aces. They are just a bunch of stumblebums."

"That doesn't give me much comfort."

"It's not supposed to. It's supposed to get you to use your giant brain to figure out your survival." Santiago wanted answers. "How about going east into Pakistan?"

"You do remember I told you that I had a penchant for burning bridges and wrecking relationships? Well, my crowning achievement was in Pakistan. I not only burned the bridge; I blew up the town. Kind of a scorched-earth campaign. If I went there, I wouldn't get across the border before I was arrested and, I'm sure, disappeared."

"Doesn't anyone like you?"

"My mother, occasionally, when I bring her gifts."

"Do you have any contacts in the stan countries?"

"No."

"You're making this hard."

"Sergeant Major, you don't have to take care of me. I created my mess—"

Santiago cut him off. "You won't get out of Afghanistan unless someone looks out for you, so spare me the strongman response. In three words, you are fucked." Santiago laughed. "Does that make sense to you?"

"It's a bit vulgar, but the meaning is clear." Bivens paused, searching for words. "If you get hooked up with me, you're going to destroy your career. You can't do that for someone you barely know. You do understand, I am always in trouble. I'd hate to stain you with it."

"You've never been in trouble like this. There are people out there with your picture looking for you so that they can make a buck by bringing in your carcass."

They fell silent and thought about what faced them.

"You write for Al Jazeera. Can I assume you have a Qatari visa along with your passport?" Santiago was trying to formulate a plan.

"That I do. Even better, the muckety-mucks at Al Jazeera want to talk to me. You see, the writing I've done about your foray into this valley has made me a hot commodity."

"Could they protect you?"

"You know, I have never had the need to think about it, but I suppose they could."

"Even more importantly, would they cover you on a flight to London?"

"Sergeant Major, what are you cooking up for me?" Bivens was curious; what the marine was talking about might be his ticket to survival.

"As I see it, the greatest danger to you will be in Afghanistan, and I think I have a way to cover you until I can get you out of the country."

"I assume somewhere in this plot you will tell me my role?"

"The marines will be pulling out of the valley in a couple of days. Right now, no one knows your location, but once we clear this place, I think people will be able to figure it out. That will expose you, at which point every asset that can be brought against you will be employed. I think what we ought to do is confuse the picture."

"Am I to dress in women's clothing and pass as your Afghan bride?"

161

"I like the idea," Santiago joked before he got back on topic. "We are going to make a very open show of your leaving this camp. I want the rescued contractors to see you drive off in your truck. I'm going to have my ordnance guy rig your truck with explosives. In the deserted stretch of the road that winds its way through the hills, you'll get out of the vehicle and move away from it, then detonate the explosives. In about two hours, I'll fabricate a report that you hit an IED. And I'll make a show of going out to look for you. I'll take a dozen marines with me. When we find the wreck, we'll photograph it, and I'll report that your truck and especially you were pulverized and that there wasn't a chunk of you large enough to recover. I'll get you back in camp. You will not leave my hut and will stay hidden until we retrograde. As we do, the first people to leave will be the contractors. They can spread the story of your demise. Perhaps, being the ones closest to you at your death, they might be able to pick up some extra dollars."

"Sergeant Major, I think I'd rather take my chances than to keep my hair this short." Bivens shook his head. "You understand that your plan is flimsy. It will never hold up to scrutiny."

"By the time people start seriously looking for holes in the story, I hope you'll be in merry old England."

"One gaping hole in your plan—and I hate to seem ungrateful for what you are trying to do for me—is that I will have to transit the Kabul airport, and I don't think a high and tight haircut is going to be enough to get me through security."

"I think I have that covered."

"Would you mind sharing the plan with me?" Bivens was uncomfortable with someone other than himself controlling his life.

"The majority of our supplies and equipment transit the major airports, but every now and then we have to run an emergency supply flight to al-Udeid in Qatar, the major US air base in this part of the world. I'll request something that can only be supplied out of Qatar, and you'll get on a marine aircraft to take the flight there in my place. Once you're on the ground in Qatar, you're on your own."

"It may be the dumbest plan I have ever heard, and for that reason I suspect it may work."

"It is not up to my usual standards of specificity, but it is the best I can come up with on short notice. Besides, you have no choice, because the next IED won't be fake." Santiago knew he had the reporter's buy-in.

CHAPTER 5

ROOKS IN DEFENSE OF THE CESSPOOL

Erik King, as he usually did when he was in Washington, scoured all the agencies to try to drum up business. His company had contracts across the span of government, and he wielded so much power that he didn't have to call for appointments; he just dropped in to see friends who funneled work his way.

Entering the office of the national security adviser, he was shocked to see the piles of papers on every surface. Stanley Weeks wasn't a computer guy. He relied on hard copy, and it showed. If there was a filing system or some arrangement to track the papers, some of which were lying on the floor, it wasn't evident. This system was antithetical to everything King believed. He was a meticulous man and could conduct his business, running an international corporation, from his smartphone.

Finding no clear path to his friend's desk, he took a seat across from Weeks without being invited to do so. Theirs was a tenuous friendship because Weeks knew his time in government service was limited, and King had dangled the possibility of hiring him at a midrange six-figure salary when the time came. He felt that he had to ignore King's rudeness because he was still in the job interview process.

"I'm glad you came here before your meeting with the president," Weeks informed King across a pile of papers.

"Well, Stan, this isn't a personal call. I came to see if I could get a piece of the action in guarding al-Bairaq oil fields. You've got the military protecting them, but it's a job ideally suited for Xyze. You could pull the military off the project, then Xyze could step in and do the job seamlessly."

Weeks wasn't in the mood to discuss anything other than the crisis he was facing. "That's something you're going to have to work out with the Pentagon. I'll surely back your assessment when it reaches me, but I have to warn you, Erik, the president is hopping mad. He had me pull up the figures on what we have spent with ISSAC in Afghanistan."

"I spoke with him two days ago, and he seemed fine with everything," King rebutted.

"That was before the reporter whom you assured him was dead turned up in London to write a feature article." Weeks was referring to an op-ed that Bivens had written for Al Jazeera's London affiliate. "I'll tell you that it's a hit piece that doesn't make Xyze look good."

"Don't sweat it. It's more fake news."

"That would be an easy explanation that would take some of the heat off, but it won't have legs. The story is damning. It's based on interviews conducted with each of the nine survivors whom the marines rescued."

"That's impossible. My people would never have spoken to a reporter."

"That may be so, but here's the article. It's supposed to be picked up by several news outlets in the United States. See for yourself and tell me what you think." Weeks handed King a copy of the article, which had been forwarded to him by the director of national intelligence. "Take time to read it before you go to see the president. He has been briefed on it and is pissed. I suppose he will take some of that anger out on you as he has already had a piece of my ass." Weeks tried to soften the blow to the man he hoped would hire him.

King read quietly. As he came to the end of the article, his normally smooth white skin was flushed.

"My people told me that this Bivens son of a bitch was killed by an IED. They wouldn't lie to me." He was searching for an answer.

"Did any of your team see the actual explosion?"

"No, but I was told they were close enough to hear it and that the marines found only the reporter's damaged truck, which they photographed. There wasn't enough left of the body to identify."

"Well, obviously something doesn't jibe. The guy is alive and has several more stories to write that will fill in all the blanks."

"I've got people in London who can make him disappear." King was calculating how he could get Bivens out of the way.

"Stop right there. There is no way you can kill a reporter in England. If that was ever discovered, it would make the massacre story look like child's play. Just ride this out. I think the most damage has already been done. The rest we can cover with a smoke screen. I've contacted Fox News, and they are ready to debunk anything Bivens says. He'll be painted as a hater of the United States, which will put a damper on a lot of what he says."

King liked his own solution better but was willing to listen. With so much on his mind, he'd forgotten that his purpose for visiting the national security adviser was to drum up business. He put that aside to try to get clues as to Baron's mood.

"When I visit the president, how will I find him?"

"Well, first thing this morning when this story started filtering in, he was volcanic. He was raging about you betraying him and was calling for the dollar amounts spent with ISSAC in Afghanistan."

"That can't be good. Did you give him the numbers?"

"I gave him a comparison of the amount spent by ISSAC versus that spent by the military. At first glance, your numbers didn't look too good, so to inflate the figures, I threw in money that the military was spending in Iraq. By comparing the inflated figures, ISSAC looks like a bargain. You're still expensive, but that won't show up in the number we've sent over to the White House."

"Thanks, Stan. When you get through with this job, I have a place for you on the board of ISSAC." It was the third time that King had intimated the same thing, so Weeks felt sure he had a job after he left the NSC.

Erik King waited anxiously for Baron to call him into the Oval Office, knowing that by making him wait, the president was sending him a message. Usually when he came to visit, he was ushered in to see Baron, bypassing dozens of people waiting. It was usual for Baron to terminate what he was doing and have King come in immediately. Waiting was a new experience, and he didn't like it. He sat quietly, not engaging with any of the others in the room.

"Mr. King," a secretary called, indicating it was his time. That was also new. Baron usually came to the door and led him into the office.

Entering, he could see the president wasn't ready for him. He was on the phone but not talking. King knew it was an act to make him uneasy. Baron waved his hand at a chair, indicating that King should sit, and with a flourish yelled something into the phone and slammed it down.

"Goddammed fake news. They make up stories to make me look bad." The president stopped the thought. "That brings me to more fake news. Tell me again how your people reported that the English reporter for Al Jazeera was blown to bits so small they couldn't be identified."

King now knew the reason for the president's ire.

"You yourself called me and reported that the Bivens guy was in so many pieces that there was no way to collect his body parts, so your people just left him. That's what you told me, wasn't it?"

"That was the information I had at that time."

"Well, it was bad information." The president threw an intelligence report at his guest. "Obviously, someone somewhere put the body parts together because the son of a bitch is going to write a follow-up series on the massacre. Your incompetence has left me with a couple of problems that I wasn't counting on."

"Mr. President, if I may?" King asked for the right to interrupt Baron's tirade.

"Go ahead, peddle some more bullshit."

"Sir, the information I gave to you was given to me by those contractors who were rescued. Obviously, they were mistaken. If you'll give me time, I'll find out why their stories are not lining up."

"Not lining up?" the president shouted. "They fucking lied to you."

"Give me a chance to see what went wrong."

"You bet I will. You're going to find out why this guy is still alive, and then you're going to shut him up."

King stopped talking, not knowing if he was receiving an order to eliminate Bivens so soon after being told by Stanley Weeks that that was out of the question.

"Are you saying that you approve my taking action against the reporter?"

"You're the contractor, the expert. Figure out what has to be done. And this time, don't fuck it up."

King was leery. He hadn't been given an order. Baron had left distance between himself and any action that might be taken and was putting King on the hook for success or failure, and for conviction if the whole thing fell apart. King had worked with the president many times and knew that was the way he operated, but this time it felt different. Holding a secret meeting while representing the president was like doing a chore. What was being proposed was murder.

King didn't feel comfortable with the vague order he'd received. He would be taking a risk for a man who he knew would dispose of him to protect himself. This made King squirm in his chair. There wouldn't be an email trail, nor would there be any evidence that the conversation had taken place. King was thinking about how he could layer people between him and the death of Bivens so, like the president, he could deny responsibility.

"You know, ISSAC and Xyze haven't done shit in Afghanistan and have made a ton of money." The president shifted his point of attention. It was his way of forcing King to do what he wanted without ever having to order him.

"I just looked over the figures for the money that has been spent on your companies since we got involved in Afghanistan. The numbers are alarming. You've raked in nearly half a trillion dollars, and all I can see that I got for that money is a massacre story. Now I'm going to have to develop cover stories to drown out the noise the reporter is making. I'm also faced with the prospect of having to negotiate for the three men you left behind. Just between you and me, do you think the money spent on your companies makes sense? Where's the bang for the buck?"

"Mr. President, ISSAC and Xyze have provided invaluable services to this country." King was on the defensive.

"Really? The military could have done the work you say you do at a cheaper cost. How did you worm your way into all these contracts?" Baron liked having King on the defensive. "I think I'm going to have my people look at the trade-offs and see where you might be replaced." The president was toying with an idea that King knew wouldn't come to fruition, but he didn't like being verbally spanked.

"Before you go off half-cocked, you'd better understand that six of the major donors to your campaign and inauguration are people and companies that hold points in ISSAC and that your sons hold points in ISSAC in your name. The points your family holds have been worth about twenty-five million dollars a year. If ISSAC starts losing money, your points will lose value, and as you know, I have the right to buy them back at what you paid for them: nothing. I don't think you'd like to see the profitability of the company go down because of a decision you make." King had referred to points because ISSAC was a privately held company. He didn't sell shares or partnerships; he tied people to the company by utilizing a point system. He retained full control and awarded investors and friends points that paid off handsomely when business was good. A point was worth a percentage of the ISSAC profits that King decided to distribute. The point holders couldn't vote and didn't have a say in the way the company was run; they just made money. For those who wanted to sell their points, they had to sell them back to ISSAC and couldn't peddle them on the open market. Somehow, King had gotten the scheme approved by the IRS and avoided SEC scrutiny because the men who headed those bureaus would be awarded a point after leaving government employment.

"Wil," King said, using the name no one else would use to show that he was in control, "you'd better think hard about cutting ISSAC off. To do so is bad for your business as well as mine."

The president leaned back in his chair and smiled, realizing that King was as cutthroat as he was. That was why he liked him. Sons of wealth, they presented themselves as hard workers, men of the people, whom they actually disliked. Knowing he was checkmated, the president switched to another topic. "Your three men held by the Taliban, how much in negotiations do you want me to give up to recover them? Because the Taliban is dangling them as bargaining chips."

"Nothing." King was cold in his assessment. "The beauty of using contractors shows in this case. If the three prisoners were military, you'd have to go through all the wailing of families asking you to do something. You don't have that with contractors. When they hire on, they become elements of production that can be written off. My advice is that if you can get them back on the cheap, you might score some PR points, but they can be lost in the grind of the war and it won't be noticed. Some of their families don't know they're prisoners. The company has no responsibility for the captives other than to terminate their contracts."

"You're a hard man, Erik."

"But I know how to make money off war."

"That's all I wanted to talk to you about. Do what you think is best." Baron dismissed King, leaving him to figure out what to do with Bivens. No matter what King decided, Baron was sure the conversation had no way of coming back to stain him.

King left the White House with all his contracts intact. During his talk with Baron, he was never worried about losing them, because ISSAC had a web of agreements with friends of the president and had Baron tied up with the cash cow from which he would never detach himself. King had listened to Baron's ranting, knowing nothing was going to change. Still, he was not used to being scolded by anyone, and the fact that he had to sit and listen to Baron rage against him had made him angry. In all his life, he had never allowed anyone to treat him that way. Knowing when going into the meeting with Baron what the outcome would be, he chaffed that he had had to sit and listen to a man who didn't have his fortune or the success that he had. King's privatization efforts across the government had made ISSAC an equal partner in the agencies it inhabited. King's success was tied to selling important members of Congress and bureaucrats on the efficiency of privatization while dangling the jobs awaiting them after public service. With such a lure, politicians and bureaucrats were amenable to having agencies privatized.

Getting on his private jet, Erik King was troubled. The president had pointed out that the reporter, the one King had reported dead, was alive and that the rescued contractors had passed on erroneous information. Priding himself on running a tight ship, where he was a phone call away from having control of every facet of his business, he wanted to get to the bottom of what went wrong. He steered his airplane to company headquarters, where he knew the nine contractors who had returned from Afghanistan were gathered. En route, he worked the phones so that he could meet with the men immediately upon landing.

A car was waiting for King. Within minutes he was in a sterile conference room, devoid of personal touches, with the nine returnees.

Taking his seat at the head of the long conference table, he was determined to find out what had gone wrong with the Bivens story. Once he got his facts straight, he would call the president with a revised report.

"Gentlemen, I have just returned from Washington, where I met with a highly agitated president. I had passed on your report about the English newspaperman's death, which, it turns out, is false. Bivens is alive and well and living in London. What I need to determine is how all the body parts that couldn't be identified reconstituted themselves in London. So how about telling me your theories on how this happened?"

The men at the table all looked at the pads of paper before them. All were reluctant to speak.

"Okay. Let's start this way." King attempted to open a dialogue. "Did any one of you see the remains of Bivens?"

A muffled "no" was the general response.

"So, none of you saw a body or body pieces. Where did you get your information?"

All the contractors said that they had relied on what the marines who went out to investigate the IED explosion had told them.

"Did any of you personally question the marines who did the investigation?" King couldn't believe that his professionals had been so shoddy. "You guys were part of an elite team that was picked to do two jobs: get us into a war and kill Bivens. All you accomplished was getting involved in a massacre, which in essence prevented us from widening the war, and you missed on Bivens. That is not the way Xyze conducts business. We tell the government that we can do specific jobs better than anyone in government. That's why they pay us big bucks; that's why I pay you big bucks. You let me down." What King didn't mention was that he was going to fire every one of them once he had had a chance to do a deeper investigation into what went wrong. He couldn't break the news to them because he needed their silence, which he could only ensure if they remained on the payroll.

The meeting went on for over an hour, and King kept getting hints, from what the contractors said, that there may have been some marine effort in steering his men off course. They explained that as part of their release, they had to talk to a French psychiatrist, before loading onto marine vehicles. King was appalled to learn a psychiatrist was involved. Now he understood how Bivens had gotten the intimate details he had outlined in his story. He made the tie to Bivens immediately. His men had told their stories to the reporter, and he surmised that was the reason Bivens's story had details that it would be impossible for him to know in any other context. The contractors hadn't made the connection, but King had, and that meant Bivens had more information than had been reported and could continue writing about the massacre, keeping it in people's minds.

There was a link that King drew to the marines. The psychiatrist could have been planted only with the marines' help, and the report of Bivens's death by the marines must have been false. King had to determine why the marines had become accomplices in a scheme that might hurt Xyze's bottom line.

He dismissed the contractors and was on the phone to the headquarters of the marine corps. Determined to get to the bottom of what had happened with Bivens, he was thinking that the marines' inability to provoke a larger war might be tied up in one package.

With his connections, King had no difficulty getting a look at private files of the marines assigned to the Zukan Valley, knowing that any fight that they might have provoked would have trapped them between the Taliban and the might of US airpower. A few

US marine deaths in an epic battle were figured into the planning, and King knew that the unit that only contained enlisted men was expendable.

In Monday morning quarterbacking, he visualized the entire scenario, but he couldn't understand how enlisted men on the ground and near the fight had managed to pull off the stalemate that got Xyze involved. He didn't bother to look at the enlisted men but focused on the battalion from which they came. He wanted to determine if it was the officers who had put the plan together—because he didn't think enlisted personnel could do it.

As King scoured the information that the US Marine Corps had provided, one name stood out, that of Sergeant Major Jaio Santiago. When King first saw the name, it didn't make an impression on him, but all the significant events in the valley had Santiago's fingerprints on them. King wasn't willing to believe that an enlisted man, especially an assumed Latino, could be cunning enough to turn off the air war, so he searched higher up in the chain of command for an officer who might have pulled the strings. He found no officer. Santiago had been sent to the valley as the commander, which was unusual, and seemed to have been given the responsibility and authority to conduct operations there. Of course, he had to report back to higher headquarters, but he was cut loose from the chain of command and had to report only to Dunne and Waddle at the NSC, which created confusion, cutting out marine headquarters.

The evidence King was gathering pointed to the sergeant major. Reluctantly, he decided to take a deeper dive into background of the enlisted man. He was going to find out if Santiago was the reason Xyze had come off looking as bad as it had.

King looked at the reports Santiago filed daily and saw that the marines had patrolled aggressively. They went out daily looking for the fight that would allow the air war to start, but wherever they patrolled, the Taliban didn't engage them. It was the lack of contact that had gotten Xyze involved. They had sold themselves as a unit capable of finding the Taliban and drawing them into a battle. They're the ones who had set the course for finally leaving Afghanistan. King didn't want to admit that in order to do that, Xyze had gone over the top and conducted a brutal massacre, killing women and children, a debacle that he himself had become ensnared in by trying to hide it under the cover of an act of war. The English reporter had blown up the agreed-upon PR strategy.

While King was studying Santiago, he latched onto the relationship between the marine and the reporter. The Englishman had gotten himself close to all the action, and that could have occurred only if he had been given access by the marine sergeant major. The fact that Bivens had been passed off as a psychiatrist and was given access to all the recovered Xyze personnel individually could only have been set up with Santiago's go-ahead.

King didn't make a request that some action be taken against Santiago through normal channels. He got on the phone with the secretary of defense.

After clearing the wickets to speak to the secretary, King didn't waste time with formalities. He flew to Washington and walked into the office of the secretary of Defense unannounced.

"David." He identified the secretary of defense David Thorn, the CEO of a major defense contractor who was on leave of absence to serve in the government. King knew him from past business dealings where Thorn's company had held significant points in ISSAC. In a sweetheart deal, King bought hardware from Thorn's company and monopolized the market for certain types of drones. In turn, Thorn's company made a profit off the sales and off the points it owned in ISSAC. King and Thorn had worked out the details personally, and both considered it a win-win situation.

"I need a favor." King didn't waste time in getting to the purpose of his visit.

"Sure, what can I help you with?" Thorn knew King wouldn't propose something that was illegal.

"I've been trying to break some personnel records out of the marine corps, and they are citing privacy rules. They have given me a series of requirements I have to fulfill to get the records. Honestly, I don't have the time, so I was wondering if you could break the logjam and get them for me."

"If they aren't classified, that won't be a problem." Thorn was curious. "What is it that you're looking for?"

"As you well know, Xyze has not come out of Afghanistan looking good."

"That's an understatement." Thorn tried to make a joke.

"Well, I think I have found what might be the reason for the failure and the bad press."

"We've written it off in the Pentagon as fake news."

"That works for a lot of things, but the president is making noise about cutting off ISSAC from a lot of government work. So, fake news or not, the stories—and I'm led to believe more will be coming—have the potential of hurting our bottom line." King inferred that once Thorn got back to his old job, the profitability of his company could be hurt because its ISSAC points wouldn't be paying as well.

Further explanation wasn't required. Thorn, as CEO, had pushed his company into a relationship with ISSAC. It was a controversial move for a defense contractor, and he'd faced opposition from his own board of directors. He had won the battle, but if ISSAC profitability were to tank, his company's bottom line would be affected, so even as he served as the secretary of defense, he was looking to the job he would be returning to, wanting his transition to be seamless.

"Here's what I need you to do." King didn't mask his intent. "Cut back on your investigation into Xyze and the massacre, and shift the focus to the marines. It was, after all, their failure to goad the Taliban into the air war that necessitated the insertion of Xyze. I want you to find out why the marines couldn't find a fight, and figure out some spin that will exonerate Xyze. I think the massacre can be buried in a report that will shift the blame to the marines' lack of action. Put out reams of information so that there will be ample confusion to deflect the blame. You shouldn't have to prove their failure. All we want to do is muddy the waters so that the president will forget about cutting off any ISSAC contracts. This war will end soon, and the troops will be pulled out, but there is going to be an increased need for the things ISSAC and Xyze can do in that country."

Thorn understood that the war would end and that ISSAC intended to take over all the in-country functions of the military. They would increase their workforce, placing as many contractors on the ground as the military personnel they replaced. A name was already being floated for what their mission would be called. It would be a lot more expensive than having the military do the job, but it would be money spent off the books. The costs of the war could be hidden, and the United States could expand its mercenary forces and operate without the inconvenience of government oversight.

Thorn wasn't uncomfortable with what he was being asked to do. He was taking orders from a person who received no oversight from the government. His only restraint was the president. He wondered if he was violating the oath he'd taken upon being sworn in to head up the DoD. It was a quick thought. When he had talked his board of directors into upping its stake in ISSAC, he was aware of the postwar plans for Afghanistan. There was going to be a lot of money made, and when he compared the oath he had uttered with his hand on the Bible, he found that the words seemed insignificant, because in Washington words were cheap and only money talked.

King seemed happy with the conversation. Thorn would do whatever he was asked or told to do. "Now, keep your investigation of the marines low-key. If word gets out that you're investigating the military, all hell will break loose. To start, don't report this out to anyone but me. When I have a chance to shape the narrative, I'll get the story to the president, then he can leak it to the news if he thinks he can get some mileage out of it." King stood to leave. His business was done and he had other officials to see in the capitol.

Thorn was left to figure out how aggressively he wanted to carry out an investigation into the marine corps. He had to be careful. He headed a Defense Department that he was trying to hold together as there were many people who thought the president's actions in regard to Afghanistan were dangerous. He had weeded out many of those who voiced dissent, but they were bureaucrats, people he could afford to lose. Those he couldn't lose were the troops, and if he started an investigation into their actions, there was a real possibility they would balk. And while it was all well and good to privatize the war, contractors didn't do the dirty work on the battlefield. The troops were needed to keep the public's interest in any war the United States engaged in. They were the dressing that allowed the public to rationalize that the country had a representative army. While the public accepted the ease of fighting wars with mercenaries, it was the public relations piece about the sons and daughters who shed blood that received the news that allowed Americans to hide under rocks and think that what was happening was normal.

The battalion was reconstituted with the return of Santiago's troops. Now they were waiting in their sparse camp for orders to leave Afghanistan. With little to do, as most of their gear had been packed, their one form of entertainment available was to spread rumors about when they would actually depart. Every marine knew someone with inside information who had told him what was about to happen; rumors swirled through the camp like information tornadoes. There was nothing to grab onto, and the shelf life was only as long as it took for the next rumor to get caught up in the wind.

Sergeant Major Santiago had been involved in too many deployments and retrogrades to listen to anything. He was as anxious to leave as his marines were, but he had learned that nothing was final until a hard copy of the orders to move out had been delivered. He waited for that to happen in his hut, sitting at his desk, running over the events he had recently survived in his head. He understood just how lucky he was to have stumbled onto Bivens, and he realized that it was the newspaperman and the power of the pen that had averted a sure catastrophe. He didn't know how many lives would have been chewed up in the air war, but he guessed thousands. He was sure that among those deaths would have been many of the marines sent as sacrificial lambs. He smiled at the good fortune of having worked with Bivens to get the story about what was happening and what had happened in the Zukan out ahead of the decision makers in Washington. It was Bivens's powerful words, funneled through a media organization looked at skeptically in the United States, that had forestalled the big war.

His reverie was interrupted. "Sergeant Major, Colonel Keefe would like to see you." It was in the form of a request, but Santiago pushed back from his desk, knowing he had received an order.

He walked across an open area in which gritty, sand-laden air swirled, dirtying his clean utility uniform.

"Ice. Come on in and take a seat. I have to talk to you." Santiago sat across from the colonel. "I've got some bad news."

The words caught Santiago's attention. He had no idea what the news might be.

"The retirement papers you submitted have been put on hold. Headquarters Marine Corps knows nothing about why they were sidetracked, but it appears that the secretary of defense's office has interest in you and doesn't want you off active duty when we return to the States. I wish I could tell you more, but no one in our chain of command has ever seen anything like this, especially having the secretary of defense involved."

Santiago thought he might know the reason for the special treatment, but he didn't share that speculation with his friend. If he were to tell Keefe the story, it would remove his defense of having been unaware of what had happened in the Zukan. In all the reports Santiago had filed through higher headquarters, he made sure there was distance between what he was doing and instructions from the battalion.

The secretary of defense could get anything done through the military that King couldn't get done. He received every report the marines filed in regard to the battle in the Zukan. Thorn had his top investigators pick apart every word of the voluminous document cache, which they did, ultimately unable to find any wrongdoing. It helped that no one knew what they were looking for or why. Thorn couldn't tell his staff he was having them do all the extra work as a favor to Erik King, so he put himself on the line for criticism. The report was done quickly. It now sat on the corner of his desk, waiting for him to pick it up.

Unlike other lobbyists who roamed the halls of government, King didn't need appointments. His preferred method was to walk into offices unannounced and watch the staff scramble the schedule to ensure he got right into see their bosses. Such access didn't come cheap. It was no secret across government that King could make employment after government service profitable. Everyone he dealt with knew that and courted him like a royal.

Getting to the secretary of defense took a little more time. King was forced to call ahead so that time could be made for him on the secretary's schedule. King couldn't always get the time he wanted, but he always got to see Thorn.

"I placed Mr. King on your schedule for a lunch meeting," a military aide informed Thorn. It was an imposition, but Thorn showed no anger at the interruption.

"Instead of going to the dining room, find out what Mr. King would like to eat and have it brought to the office. I'll have my usual," Thorn instructed.

"Yes, sir." The aide backed out of the office.

Thorn sat behind his desk and was glad he would be getting rid of the pile of papers that described the marines' conduct in the Zukan. The results might not be what King was looking for, but the facts indicated the marines had acted properly.

King showed up at noon and was surprised to see that he was going to have a private lunch with the secretary. He preferred going to the executive dining room, where everyone could see him leading a government official around by the nose. The display of power was good for business. With Thorn, it was a little different. He was on a leave of absence and had a job to go back to at the end of his government stint. The only leverage King had over him was the fact that Thorn as the CEO had a sizable chunk of the points offered by ISSAC.

In other words, Thorn had to be handled differently. King couldn't run over him as he did those seeking jobs.

"There's your report, all three-hundred-plus pages of it." Thorn reached across the desk and slid the stack of papers toward King.

"What did you find out? The marines didn't do their job, did they?" He hoped to put words into Thorn's mouth.

"On the contrary. All indications are that the marines performed well."

"Well, how was it that my guys could go out and find a fight when the marines couldn't? In a couple of days, Xyze found a fight and gave the United States a reason to start the air war. It doesn't make sense that the marines fumble-fucked around for weeks and came up empty."

"It might be appropriate to change your terms. Xyze didn't find a fight; they massacred nineteen women and children. There was no way we could unleash the air war based on the report of a massacre."

Without opening the report, King was sure he knew what had gone on.

"The reports I've received from my sources tell me that the warlords were told not to attack the marines." King was happy that he had channels of information outside the military.

"Who are the sources? We'll have military investigators interview them." Thorn was willing to listen. If the marines had done something wrong, he wanted to know. King seemed reluctant to answer, so Thorn asked again, "Who are the sources?"

"They're people who work for me."

"Xyze contractors?" Thorn shook his head in amusement. "Erik, they are hardly unbiased. It was Xyze who conducted the massacre, and you want to use them to vindicate the mess they created?"

"We have contacts among the warlords, who give us good information."

"How do you come by the information?"

"We pay the warlords not to attack any facility that we are guarding."

Thorn was astounded. "You're telling me that the outfit that sells itself as the world's premier security firm pays for security?" Thorn's eyes widened in disbelief. "How does that happen? I hope the contracts that you're working for the military aren't in the pay-for-security scheme, because I think that may be illegal under DoD rules."

"It isn't. We've been paying warlords since the beginning of the war."

"That doesn't make it right. It makes it terribly dangerous. We've noticed that the weapons the Taliban are getting are the best manufactured in the world. They only get those weapons if they can pay in dollars, and I assume you're paying them in dollars." Thorn thought for a moment before blurting out, "Jesus Christ, you're paying the Taliban to leave Xyze alone. Then they're using the money to buy newer weapons to kill our soldiers and marines. If that isn't illegal, it is immoral. And it would be one tough sell to the American people."

It was seldom that King didn't dominate a conversation, but faced with what Thorn had said, he seemed at a loss for words. "We're not the only ones paying for protection."

"Erik, stop. Bury your business practices and don't let them see the light of day again. If some reporter gets wind of what you've been doing, I'll have no choice but to cut you out of DoD contracts."

"And risk cheapening your investment?"

"This isn't about money." Thorn was angry that the man across from him couldn't see the political disaster that loomed if the story were to get out. "This is about having the president going before a family who just lost a son or daughter and telling them that the weapon that killed their child was most likely purchased with US dollars paid to the enemy to buy security for civilian firms."

Wanting to get away from the topic, King pivoted. "Okay, here's what I know. Minor warlords were ordered by their central authority not to attack the marines. Somewhere in that is a story of a buyout, the kind of thing you're accusing Xyze of."

"I'd be very surprised if we found out that the marines had bought off the Taliban. We have checked all the cash expended vouchers, and the largest amount spent was less than a hundred dollars. That is hardly the kind of money that would buy off the Taliban central command." Thorn couldn't see where King wanted to take the conversation by implicating the marines. "I think you'd better drop the case you're trying to make, because once that genie is let out of the bottle, there will be inquiries into who else might have paid the Taliban—and that stink is going to attach itself to Xyze. Even worse, it requires that I look into all contracts with Xyze, and if DoD money was spent, I'm afraid there would be an across-the-board voiding of all contracts. Neither of us needs the bad publicity that would bring."

"The marines had to have bought off the Taliban." King was unwilling to let go of his idea.

"Have you discussed this with anyone else?" Thorn was getting into the specifics.

"The president and several close associates."

"And you think this story won't leak? Erik, wake up. This is Washington. People will be waking up in the morning to read all about this in the *Washington Post*." Thorn switched topics, wanting to get to the nub of his problem. "What was the president's reaction?"

"He agrees with me. He thinks that if the marines had done their job, the air war would be over and we'd be preparing to leave Afghanistan. He's in favor of an investigation into what went wrong."

"He hasn't indicated that to me."

"He will. I have a meeting with him this afternoon. I'll be sure to have him call you." King was smug, knowing that he was going to sell his plan to the president.

"I can see that I can't talk you out of this, but I'll caution you one last time: if this story breaks, it will be bad for the country and bad for Xyze. It is going to hurt Xyze's reputation and could place you on the outside of the decision-making loop."

"The marines pulled some trick. I can feel it in my bones. If they did, someone has to pay for it. We need a fall guy to make this story disappear."

"Massacres don't vanish. And the people who conducted the massacre were your contractors. Erik, you have the investigation the Pentagon conducted into the marines' actions in the Zukan. When you are pitching the president, be sure to tell him that we found nothing amiss. In that report, no mention was made of Xyze, but if you keep stirring the pot, you're going to get dirty." Thorn pushed back from his desk, indicating the meeting was over.

King didn't know what to do. He was unused to being treated so ordinarily when he dealt with bureaucrats. He gathered the report and left as Thorn took a phone call.

⁓

Before going to the White House, King took a side trip. For a man who loved the display of power and wanted to be seen with the movers and shakers in the best eateries in town, his descent into a coffee shop was out of character. He occasionally slummed, as he referred to it, when he had sensitive information to pass on to his subordinates. The people whom he was going to meet worked for him, but there was no paper trail showing that they did. They were from the Xyze special ops group, a group within the ISSAC organization that few people knew existed. They themselves would not get their hands dirty with the sometimes grisly world of special ops, but they knew how to layer people between the job they were tasked to do and themselves. By the time they got done putting firewalls around Erik King, there was no way anything could be traced back to him.

Two men were seated at the lunch counter. When King approached them, one stood and moved to the drugstore's entrance. He served as a watchful guard to ensure the conversation that was going to take place at the counter was private. It was also a precaution that King took to ensure that only a few people were involved in what he was doing.

"Thanks for meeting me on such short notice," he said, greeting Marty Hogan.

"No sweat, Mr. K." Hogan was an ashen man with deep-set eyes that didn't focus on the man he was talking to. His eyes roamed the lunch counter, looking for perceived threats. He was a sinister man who lived in a world of his own making, always seeing danger.

"Is everything in place for the London job?"

"Yes, sir. I spoke to the operators this morning. All they need is the okay to proceed. That and a bag full of cash."

"Have you checked over their plan? Their last attempt at wiping out a threat didn't come off smoothly. Scotland Yard almost nailed them before they escaped. Do you feel confident using these guys?"

"They've formed a new team, and I've looked over their plan. It's tight. There will be no mistakes."

"How about any links to ISSAC?"

"This can't be tied to us. The money won't leave any tracks that can be followed. I'll deliver dozens of payments of cash to our offshore banks. That money will be spun through two other offshores before it is transferred to an Icelandic bank. That is the first time the money will be put together for payment. It will be the final wash before putting it in the Swiss system. A numbered account is in place from which the operatives can withdraw the money without a trace. We have put the extra transfers in so that all the money will be clean. There is no way to link it to us."

"Do you feel good about this getting done right?" King asked, posing a hard question to his subordinate. If something were to go wrong, he would have someone to blame other than himself.

"I've been involved with several of these, and this is as tight as they come. Don't you sweat the details; that's my job. I'll get this done for you without fingerprints." Hogan was proud of the web of people he had put together with none of them knowing whom he or she was working for other than the person they were dealing with. "All we need, Mr. King, is the order to execute."

King was hesitant. He didn't care about Bivens. Bivens was merely an obstacle to be removed. King knew that by keeping his distance from the operation and putting his faith in others to carry it out, there might be lack of attention to detail. As Hogan had never let him down, he decided it was time to act. "Go for it. And I don't want to hear another thing about it." The words seemed to lift the weight off him. When it was over, he would have some good news for the president, who he was sure would return the favor by ordering the marines to find a fall guy.

King left the coffee shop for his meeting at the White House.

———

King entered the Oval Office while the president was finishing up a photo op with farmers. After handshakes and photos, the farmers were unceremoniously directed out of the office to have cake and cookies with the vice president.

"Sit down, Erik," the president directed. "I hope you brought me some good news?"

"I think so. The London thing is taken care of." He didn't mention Bivens, and he referred to what was to take place in nebulous terms so that both men would have plausible deniability.

"This isn't going to be another Xyze foul-up that I have to cover up, is it?"

"Mr. President, you're going to see how professionals operate. This isn't going to be some half-baked operation by the CIA or the FBI. The best professionals will get this done without a trace. The target will go away and there won't be a fingerprint, a strand of DNA, nothing. Poof, the problem will be over."

The president smiled. He liked what he was hearing. By taking the assassination outside the government, he wouldn't have to worry about leaks or some government employee getting moralistic and spilling the beans. "Do you have a time line, an end date when I can consider this over?"

"Not yet, but I will have one in a couple of days and will get it to you."

"What does taking care of this thing cost? And where will you get the money? I assume you can't contract this out through normal channels." Baron related every function to money.

"Money won't be a problem. Consider this as ISSAC's gift to you. The funds will come out of an account that I keep for emergencies such as this."

"Good thinking. What's the payback you want for such generosity?"

"This is a straight gift to you to repay you for the things you've done for me and my companies." King let the words fill the room before continuing. "There is one small favor, though, that I'd like to ask."

"If it's a small one, it will get done."

"It is, Mr. President. No money is involved. I just need you to direct Don Thorn to order the marines to open a court-martial on the marine commander who failed to get us into the war we had planned on."

"Where are you going with this?"

"I've read the investigative report the DoD did on the marines, and it looks like a whitewash." King hesitated before selling his argument. "You'll remember, the marines were placed in the Zukan."

"Where?" The president was confused, not knowing what King was talking about.

"You directed that the marines in Afghanistan position a team in the heart of opium country to engage the Taliban so that we would have a pretext to wipe them out through an air war."

"Oh." It was as if Baron was trying to remember the conversation King was telling him about.

"The marines sat on their hands and did nothing for almost a month, before we decided to put a Xyze team into the valley to get the pretext for war. If the marines had done their job, there would have been no need for Xyze and there would have been no massacre. What I want done is to expose the marine inactivity and, in so doing, take the heat off Xyze. Basically, if I can spread the blame, I might get Xyze out of this without too much damage to its reputation."

"But it was your people who killed the civilians."

"We're not sure of that yet. We may find that among the people killed there were Taliban fighters."

"Are you going to use your own facts?"

"We are beginning to pick up indications that there were Taliban fighters among those killed."

The president smiled, knowing that there was no lie that couldn't be justified if one only persisted in repeating it.

"What is it that you're trying to accomplish?"

"If the case can be made that the marines were derelict in their duties, we can expand the circle of blame. Instead of people only talking about Xyze and its acts, they will always have a doubt that if the marines had done their duty, perhaps there would have been no massacre."

"For calling Don Thorn and telling him to do as you suggest, what do I get out of it? You know, I'm supposed to be the military's friend."

"It's a favor—personal favor—I'd like granted."

"Okay." Baron smiled, liking the idea of having King beholden to him. "I'll call Don and tell him to keep you in the loop. But at the first sign that your plan is coming off the track, I'm cutting you loose."

"That's fair."

They talked for a while longer. Baron was interested in King's assessment of the world, which he trusted more than that of the professionals who briefed him every day.

———

Nigel Bivens settled in the quiet neighborhood of Cottsworth. It was a coincidence that it was the same community that years before had been the home of Yuri Lesvenko, a Russian defector who was poisoned and had died with suspects but no arrests. Before the police could gather all the facts and determine that the poison used was controlled by the Russian government, the suspects had flown off to Russia and personal safety. The incident was an embarrassment to the police and the British government as the case remained opened.

When Bivens, and the multitude of threats he had received and brought with him, moved to Cottsworth, police were vigilant and advised him to install cameras around his home to detect any untoward activities. It was a good idea, but Al Jazeera went overboard in trying to protect the reporter who had made them the major news source in covering the United States' attempt to expand the Afghan War. Where Nigel had hired a firm to install cameras that were bulky and could be seen easily from the street, a deterrent in its own right, which experts could easily counter, Al Jazeera installed minicameras with state-of-the-art technology that had full night vision capabilities. They thought the investment was prudent.

Bivens, with his reporting on the war, had made them a news outlet to be contended with, especially in Great Britain, where the news had been controlled for hundreds of years by the staid establishment outlets. Bivens's writing made Al Jazeera a competitor, to the chagrin of news organizations that ignored the war in Afghanistan despite the fact that there were British troops dying in the fight. Unlike the bulky cameras hanging off the side of Bivens's home, the minicams had battery packs so that countermeasures could not take all of them off-line.

Nigel's job was to look at the camera recordings before leaving the house each morning and again when returning from work each evening, something he did willingly as the threats on his life were increasing. Looking through the tapes while having his morning tea, he discovered the system he had installed had been taken off-line. A power failure had blacked out the system. It gave him an uneasy feeling, so he scoured the tapes provided by the battery-powered minicams.

He could see two men, one wearing hazmat gloves and a protective face shield, appearing to paint the steering wheel of his car, which was parked inside his picket fence and up along the side of his house. As the men closed the door, they made a special effort to paint the door handle, something Bivens would have to touch to gain entry to the car. It only took a little over a minute, and once the job was done, the man under the protective shield raised the shield and stretched his neck so that the cameras had a full-on shot of his face.

Bivens had lost his nonchalance about being killed. In Afghanistan he had taken risks, but at home, in civilized society as he referred to it, he understood the threat was greater. Calling the police and telling them what he had recorded, he received an immediate response. Within ten minutes, hazmat teams and investigators were looking at the tapes. Many of the officers who had responded were still smarting from their failure in the Lesvenko case and wanted a chance to redeem themselves. While hazmat personnel worked over the car and finally trucked it away to a laboratory, investigators were looking at the tapes and the faces of the men. They were Russians whom Scotland Yard had on its watch list. Knowing that if they let the men fly out of the country they would end up with another cold case, they alerted Heathrow Airport. It was a fortunate call because the men were stopped prior to boarding a flight that would carry them to the safety of Russia.

With two suspects in custody, the difficult part of the investigation started. Analyzing the substance that had been slathered in and around Bivens's car was tedious work, made more time-consuming by the fact that the substance could be deadly. The utmost care had to be exercised in its handling. The two men who had been stopped at the airport were in jail, and the Russian ambassador to the United Kingdom was in a lather, trying to get them released under made-up diplomatic immunity provisions.

Gradually, a picture emerged. The attempted assassination was a carbon copy of the Lesvenko murder. A radioactive isotope, polonium-210, that which killed Lesvenko, a substance that only an atomic power plant would have, had been used in trying to kill Bivens. Trying to evoke some humor out of the situation, Nigel joked that he wasn't important enough to have a new and improved isotope used in the effort to kill him.

Thinking about the attempted assassination, Bivens tried to put the pieces together. There was a Russian attempt on his life, but why? His reporting, which informed the world of US mistakes and atrocities, had nothing to do with the Russians. In fact, it probably pleased them to see the United States taken down a peg. A Russian attempt on his life made no sense unless it entailed money. He thought about those who might have been most insulted by his reporting and could think only of Xyze. They had no reason to silence him other than to indicate to other reporters they had better be more careful in what they wrote.

As reports came to Bivens, it was determined that the assassins were in fact Russian, but they were a rogue operation. They had low-level ties to the government, but there was no discernible link to the power structure. Unable to be released to the Russian Embassy, the two men didn't like the comfort of English jails and began to talk.

Bivens's suspicions had been correct: the Russians didn't care about his Afghan reporting. The men had been hired through a shadowy network of something like killers for hire. They were usually disenfranchised special operators from around the world who sold themselves as men who would kill without conscience. They didn't know who hired them, only that the pay was good and would be doled out when the job was done.

Scotland Yard could trace the money only to the Icelandic banking system, before it disappeared in the Swiss system, where everything was locked down in secrecy.

As Bivens was the center of the story, Al Jazeera gave him an opportunity to tell it, not as a reporter with the constraints of checking out every fact, but as an opinion writer who was allowed to intersperse facts to reinforce his opinion. The piece he wrote was a bombshell. He had enough information to tie the attempted assassination to ISSAC and, hence, Xyze. There was a thread through his story that hinted the attempt on his life had been sanctioned by the US government.

He didn't have all the whys or hows, but he decided he would ferret them out.

Sitting in London offices of Al Jazeera, Bivens was surprised by an Afghan emissary from their foreign office who was allowed to travel inside England. The man was well dressed and spoke with little accent, apparently having lived in and around England for a long time.

"How can I help you?" Bivens asked after looking at his credentials and satisfying his curiosity that the man was who he said he was.

"Mr. Aziz requested that I deliver this to you." He reached into his suit jacket pocket and removed an envelope.

"What is it?"

"No one at the embassy has opened it, so I don't know."

"Are there any instructions that go along with it?" Bivens was curious. Knowing that he'd left Afghanistan without seeing Aziz or thanking him for his help, he hoped that the Afghan understood that his escape had been the act of a desperate man.

"I was told to deliver this to you." He handed the envelope to Bivens. "My job is done." As quickly as he had appeared, he was gone, leaving Bivens alone. After the attempt on his life, Bivens was cautious. He didn't know if the letter was poisoned. Since the Afghan had handled it without gloves, he assumed the exterior was clean. He laid the envelope in the center of his desk, thinking about what he should do. He thought about calling security and turning it over to them, but his curiosity got the best of him. With a letter opener and a pencil, he loosened the seal and pulled out some papers that didn't have any powder on them. Still, he wouldn't touch the contents with his bare hands, instead positioned them with the letter opener.

The interior sheet of paper was a letter addressed to him, thanking him for his efforts in preventing the air onslaught. It was a cordial letter. Bivens took it to mean more than the recognition he was receiving for his reporting. Aziz flattered him by telling him that his words might have changed the course of history. It was an honor like no other he had received, delivered from a man who had been at war for over forty years, a man Bivens respected.

After the pleasantries afforded by Aziz, the closing paragraph came with instruction, informing him that his work was not done. Aziz pointed out that though the negotiations had started again and the Americans were going to pull their troops out of his country, they had no intention of leaving. They intended to replace the military with contractors, in effect leaving Afghanistan an occupied country. Aziz requested that Bivens write about it in an effort to derail US efforts. He didn't offer much to Bivens to counter the American efforts, but the second page was a sheet torn from a ledger showing the payments made by Xyze to the Taliban for security. The circle was completed in the third page, where the money paid to the Taliban showed in the weaponry they bought internationally.

Bivens saw immediately the tie-in. The purchased weapons killed US troops. Sitting at his desk trying to piece together a story that might expose the intent of the United States in the peace negotiations, he almost ignored the fourth page. Aziz commented on Santiago's courage, indicating that an attempt wasn't going to be made on his life. Attempts would be made to ruin his reputation, and if Bivens could get the information in the letter to Aziz, it might forestall an injustice being done to an honorable man.

Bivens hadn't thought about Santiago in a while, but he immediately did a computer search and found that the sergeant major was the subject of a court-martial inquiry. Alarm bells went off in his head. He knew that if he could make a copy of the ledger page and get it to the marine, it might help him ward off those trying to destroy him.

Bivens smiled, thinking that a warlord in the middle of Afghanistan knew more about what was going on than he did, sitting in one of the world's best news-gathering organizations. He could only assume Aziz's CIA handlers were back on the job and providing him information.

A letter arrived at Camp Pendleton, California, addressed to Sergeant Major J. Santiago. Jaio noticed it as he rifled through a pile of mail that had accumulated before the court-martial was to convene. He thought it odd. He knew no one from Duneen, Scotland, and his curiosity was piqued by the name of the sender, N. B. Churchill. Knowing of only one person who would pretend to be Churchill, he opened the letter thinking he might be getting caught up on the news of his friend.

Sergeant Major,

This is not a personal note in the ordinary sense. And forgive me for having been remiss, but you see, I've been busy trying to stay alive. The idea that I would be safest in England was a myth. I was sanctioned for extinction by what appears to be US interests. Fortunately, those who were assigned to do the killing showed as much competence as the Xyze killers did in Afghanistan.

Why the subterfuge in mailing this letter, when a phone call would have sufficed? All my electronic communications devices are being monitored, as is all my mail. Some agency of your government is trying to find out what I know. Since my secretary was going to Duneen for the weekend, I had her post this letter there. If it gets to you, I will assume the contents are intact, but upon receiving it, please call me at the following number and leave a message so I will know that this part of what I am attempting to do is done.

Worried about myself, I forgot about you after our quick separation, until our friend Aziz reminded me that you had a stake in this play. While you won't be slated for termination as I was, the means that will be used to destroy you and besmirch the marine corps is a more subtle game. From my research—and I have access to the best sources Al Jazeera can buy—I found the court-martial you will be undergoing is going to try to muddy the waters in order to prove that marine culpability, your culpability, in not finding a way to start the war was the reason Xyze was brought onto the scene. The case will be made that if you had acted, there would have been no need for contractors and that you are in fact, by failing to start the war, the reason they committed their atrocity. It is not logical or legal, but if enough alternative facts are presented with you in the center, blame sharing will be presented to the American public. It's a case of damaging the good men, you marines, who held off the dogs of war.

Now the most important part of this letter is the enclosure. Aziz sent me a page of his ledger that incriminates Xyze as war profiteers. The entries on the pages show who was paid how much money and where the money was spent. You can follow the money trail from Xyze to Taliban warlords, who in turn purchased weapons good enough to counter US firepower. As you will see, many of the purchases of weapons were made from US gun manufacturers with ties to ISSAC. The ledger page shows a full cycle of money and war profiteering.

Look at the copies of the two pictures enclosed. They show groups of Taliban showing off their new weaponry.

Aziz sent me the originals of what you have. He wants me to write a story that will expose the Americans because he knows that replacing the military through negotiations with contractors will essentially mean his country will be colonized for the next hundred years—and he wants to throw that yoke off. Although he makes his money in legal and illegal ways, he has no respect for the US model, where money is a religion.

That's all I wanted to pass on to you. I know you're smart and will figure out a way to use the information in this letter.

I may never reach the stature of my hero, but if I write a strong enough story, perhaps I'll be remembered.

N.B.

———

The court-martial was convened at the battalion's California base. Unlike other high-profile judicial proceedings, which were held at the newly refurbished base headquarters building, the trial was scheduled to be held at Camp San Mateo, a remote camp on the sprawling base. It was about a twenty-minute ride from the power structure of Camp Pendleton, home of the First Marine Division. The secrecy surrounding a court-martial that otherwise was common knowledge whetted the curiosity of reporters from as far away as San Francisco, who could smell a cover-up. Descending on the base, they were given the flimsy excuse that the court-martial would be covering sensitive material, and for that reason they had to be excluded from the proceedings. That didn't sit well, nor did the fact that they'd been told they would receive a press briefing at the end of the proceedings. Reporters who had Camp Pendleton as their beat, and therefore had contacts all over the base, were denied access to the trial because they didn't have the proper clearances. Not liking what they were being subjected to, the reporters came close to rioting in trying to gain access, but not nearly as vigorously as the marines stationed on the base, who sensed what was happening to one of their own.

The San Mateo site had been selected by the lawyers from ISSAC who were assigned to assist the trial counsel, a young officer who, it was felt, with their help, could bring the case to the verdict that ISSAC desired. Two teams of lawyers from five name powerhouse firms located in Washington, DC, and San Diego controlled everything down to the times and the witness lists. The marine appointed as trial counsel was window dressing and had been given the script ISSAC lawyers wanted followed.

The stage was set, but finding the actors to fill the roles proved difficult. It was going to be a general court-martial with seven marines sitting in judgment of Sergeant Major Santiago. The first problem encountered was that Santiago was an enlisted man. The rules of general court-martial dictated that an enlisted man of commensurate rank sit on the judging panel. It was a rule imposed to limit officer-enlisted bias and ensure the enlisted defendant wasn't gamed. Although the command had searched for another sergeant major to serve, they couldn't find one. Every sergeant major who had served in Afghanistan, and that was most aboard the base, refused to serve as a member of the court. Santiago had a legendary status among the sergeants major who had served in combat, and none would accept the orders to judge him in what they considered a sham trial. With the command trying to force reluctant sergeant majors to serve, they received a surprise when two immediately retired. All others who had been approached had expressed their displeasure with what was happening and indicated they had already made a judgment. In reading the charges against Santiago, it could be seen that the language was hostile to the marines and barely mentioned Xyze or the massacre. Every marine who had served in Afghanistan understood that they were all going to be made to look bad to cover the criminal actions of contractors.

Finally, a master gunnery sergeant, a rank equal to sergeant major, was flown in from the Pentagon. Master gunnery sergeants were technical experts. The person chosen had never set foot in Afghanistan, having spent his time teaching in classrooms while the war was going on. It was another slap in the face to war fighters.

Finding officers to sit on the board proved as difficult. Santiago had served with many of the officers who had siphoned through the war, and in many cases he had mentored them. All of them claimed they had prejudged Santiago's innocence so that they wouldn't have to serve. Six officers were selected from other West Coast bases to serve, knowing that they themselves were entering a hostile environment, being judged as they themselves were judging.

With the confusion surrounding the start of the court, there were leaks daily, which made the crowd of reporters looking for a story more intent on finding out what was taking place.

Camp San Mateo was manned by a small support crew who took care of the grounds until units descended upon it for short training periods. It was out of sight and out of mind for the most part and had been selected because it would be easier to block out press coverage. It had a single gate, and no reporters were on the access list. As a final censor, all personnel who entered the camp during the trial sessions had to leave their cell phones at the gate. For young marines, for whom cell phones were a part of their lives, the separation of man and machine didn't upset them because they knew that San Mateo's remote location, deep in a box canyon, had no cell phone reception anyway.

The trial counsel, sent in from the Judge Advocate's Office in Washington, huddled with the high-priced lawyers who had been assigned to guide him. He wore a uniform with rows of medals, thinking it would help him speak to the officers sitting in judgment. Several officers comprising the board had earned their medals and knew that among the medals the counsel wore for service in Afghanistan was one earned for an overnight stay in Kabul, made purposely so that he would qualify for the award. For officers who had been shot at, seeing the counsel wear the same medal was a slap in the face.

They disliked the lawyer who was bringing a case against one of their own—that and the idea that the trial counsel had a support team of four lawyers paid for by ISSAC to move him around and make his case. For the lawyers who wore thousand-dollar suits and had hundred-dollar haircuts, the trial setting in a World War II vintage Quonset hut was dank. The hut, with dust suspended in the air and no air-conditioning, was hot and unbearable, as were the fleas and roaches that had had years to establish a habitat. As an accommodation to the lawyers who weren't used to working in difficult conditions, fans were brought in to provide some relief, but difficulty arose when the fans stirred up more dust and blew briefing papers off the tables. The fans weren't quiet. In order to generate cooling, they had to be set on high. The noise generated made normal conversation difficult. For the lawyers who were used to climate-controlled spaces, the hot, dusty environment was chafing, as were the fleas that somehow found their way onto exposed skin.

The trial counsel's opening statement was quick and to the point. He would prove that Sergeant Major Santiago deliberately undermined the mission he had been assigned. After a flourish of words to the judging panel, the trial counsel turned the court over to Santiago's defense counsel.

The defense counsel was a young captain who had no trial experience. He was a grunt who had been assigned the job and had to read up on how to conduct a court-martial defense. Both he and Santiago wore utilities, a uniform more suited for Camp San Mateo than the class A uniforms with heavy jackets and ties that the board wore. The breach in the court-assigned uniform was overlooked because everyone was suffering in the heat and the president of the court wanted to get the trial started.

"The defense has no statement to make at this time."

Santiago didn't seem disturbed by the lack of an oratorical flourish in his defense. He smiled as he whispered something into the captain's ear. The court, made up of officers from the around the marine corps, knew of his reputation as the Iceman and could see it on display. He was unfazed.

The opening gambit by the trial counsel was to portray the naming of the marine outposts in the Zukan as an act of defiance. To prove their point, they called Private Frenchie, who turned out to be a poor witness. He made the defense's case, testifying that the naming of the outposts had been part of a pool of bets and that he had picked the most unlikely names in an effort to make some cash. The harder the trial counsel and his high-priced team tried to press the case, the more innocent Private Frenchie appeared to be. The lawyers assisting the trial counsel were used to looking at jurors, in this case the panel of officers, and they could see that pushing the private and trying to get him to blunder into a statement that would incriminate Santiago was a losing proposition. Abruptly, Private Frenchie was no longer important.

When it was the defense's turn to take on the private, they declined the opportunity.

The trial counsel went through three more marines who had been with Santiago in the Zukan to little avail. Then the lawyers advising the trial counsel told him to stop trying to build a case and to begin attacking Santiago outright.

The sergeant major was sworn in. Although his defense counsel had provided no defense, he didn't look worried.

"Did you have a meeting with Hekter Aziz when you first arrived in the valley?" The question was intended to shake him.

"Yes, sir, I did."

"At that time, did you discuss not engaging the Taliban you had been sent to the valley to ferret out?"

"Not exactly."

"You seem to be evading the question. What did you talk about?"

"Aziz told me about the plans to use the marines as bait to start an air war. Which I thought odd. I had been briefed just several days earlier, in a highly classified briefing, about what was to happen, and Aziz had more details than those provided in the brief. He had received his information from the CIA"—Santiago paused for a long time—"and from Xyze contractors, who were paying him for protection. The security contractors were paying him to lay off their operations." Santiago pulled out the sheets Bivens had sent him. "This document is a copy of a page from the ledger Mr. Aziz, the magistrate for the area and Taliban leader, kept, recording his dealings with the Americans. This a copy forwarded to me by an English reporter, who has retained the original. It follows one transaction from start to finish. Xyze paid a Taliban tribal warlord leader, Gamal Kabil, eighty thousand US dollars not to attack them as they provided security for a road construction project. The document shows Kabil paying 15 percent of the amount he received to Mr. Aziz, who is the overboss of most of the Taliban in the Zukan. Mr. Kabil then took a cut and returned the money to Xyze so that they could purchase weapons for him. The money trail goes from Xyze to ISSAC and their arms-procuring division, where AR-15s, the same weapon used by our troops, are purchased. The document shows that the Taliban paid three hundred dollars a weapon for the exact weapon for which ISSAC charges the US government seven hundred fifty dollars. The weapons were delivered to Mr. Kabil, who in turn armed his troops. About two weeks after this transaction, an army supply convoy was attacked by the Kabil group. Three soldiers were killed and several were wounded. If I may, I'll present this document to the court."

The trial counsel didn't understand the significance of what he had heard, but the lawyers advising him did. They understood the copied figures could never be made available to the public. They leaned in toward the trial counsel and ordered him to file a motion stating that in light of the new information, all charges be dismissed. Since the president of the board was looking for after-retirement employment at ISSAC, he took his cue from the lawyers and terminated the trial.

The courtroom was abuzz with activity, but there was a furious rush by the ISSAC lawyers to get to Santiago.

"We are going to need any records you have, Sergeant Major, because while it may no longer be a piece of evidence in this trial, it could play in future prosecutions."

"I can't do that. On advice of counsel"—Santiago pointed to the captain who'd been sent to defend him—"the records will be given to the Marine Historical Society. Who knows, in a hundred years they may become important."

The lawyers didn't want to argue after suffering what they considered a trial defeat. As cell phone service at Camp San Mateo was nonexistent, they raced to the main base, where they could alert the world that there might be trouble brewing. They had to call their home offices to tell them to alert Erik King.

The reporters waiting around for a story knew they had one by looking at the frightened looks of the lawyers who wanted to quickly depart the base.

CHAPTER 6

NO CHECKMATE—
THE GAME GOES ON

The president, listening to the briefing officer about the possible fallout of the failed court-martial, managed to hide his anger, but once only his closest aides were in the room with him, he exploded much like Bivens's story. He hated the fact that a nobody, a man he didn't know, could threaten his reputation. He didn't care that the US government might not come off looking good; he was worried about how this might affect him personally. After the initial emotional eruption, he seethed that he was in a situation where he might have to protect his image.

Trying to vent his rage, he reached out to those who had been responsible for the mess. First and foremost was Erik King. He had promised the president that the "thing" would be taken care of professionally, better than anything any government agency could do. There would be no fingerprints and no way to trace it back to ISSAC—and impossible to implicate the government—but Bivens, the man who was supposed to be dead, was doing just that, implicating the government. Baron hadn't read Bivens's opinion piece, but he'd been briefed, and there were enough tentacles exposing plans to privatize the war though the negotiations that he knew the story had to be tamped down. When the story of the Santiago court-martial broke, the reporters who had been locked out of the proceedings weren't gentle in their treatment of Xyze. The idea of contractors paying for protection and endowing the Taliban with the ability to buy weapons that would kill US troops wasn't playing well and had to be spun. Baron wasn't concerned that the price paid for the weapons by the military was substantially higher than ISSAC was charging the Taliban. He focused on PR disasters that had to be dealt with. No one had an idea how to attack the problem.

Usually, when the president aired his grievances to his staff, he was in ass-chewing mode, but today he seemed restrained. All the blunders had been made by Erik King, who was a friend and confidant who had enough knowledge of the workings of the administration to be an embarrassment if he were implicated in the schemes. He had to be handled differently. In fact, the entire ISSAC and Xyze involvement in the wars in Iraq and Afghanistan had to be handled differently. The public couldn't find out that there were more contractors in those countries than there were military and that it had been planned to keep mercenary forces in place long after the last troops left under the fanfare that the wars had been won and there was no longer a need for US ground troops. It was a shell game played by the government, and had been for a long time, with Congress's consent. War was a moneymaker for everyone except the eighteen- and nineteen-year-old kids who got maimed. They were the chips on the table that were turned into cash.

Baron wasn't thinking about the war and its costs or how mercenaries had changed the American ethos. He was in survival mode and had to beat back the bad press he could see coming his way.

When King received a call from the president's chief of staff telling him to show up in the president's office, he knew trouble was brewing. He couldn't remember the last time the president hadn't called him directly. It was a signal being sent, and he knew how to read it. He wasn't angry at being ordered by someone other than the president, because he hadn't delivered on his promise to take care of the thing in London and was responsible for the botched court-martial. Baron had granted him a favor by allowing the court-martial to take place, but King had messed that up. The president didn't know which failure upset him more.

It was an odd meeting. There was no one in the room with the two men to take notes or record their conversation. It was understood that their words would not escape the Oval Office.

"You've put us in a very difficult position." Baron stressed *us*, when it was really King's problem.

"Yes, sir. I'll take full responsibility for the Bivens failure. I was told that the people who would be used were the best, but it turned out they weren't very good at all."

"I'm not worried about the Englishman as much as I'm worried about the total mess you've created. In going after the marine sergeant major—I don't know what you were thinking."

"I was trying to show that the marines didn't do the job they were sent to do and that it was their failure that led to the introduction of Xyze. I thought that if I could develop a counternarrative, I could dilute the blame and whitewash the massacre." King was being honest.

"Did you do any research into the guy you tried to screw?" Baron asked.

"I didn't think that was important. He was just an enlisted man who, I assumed, was in over his head."

"You should have looked into him before you tried to screw him. Right about where you're sitting, I presented him with a medal for heroism, his third such medal, and I made a speech about how he was the best this country has to offer. The son of a bitch is one of the most decorated people to come out of Afghanistan, and you tried to smear him." Baron paused. "But I don't really give a shit about that. What I do care about are the optics. I called the son of a bitch a hero, and you tried to take him down as a traitor. That makes me look bad. If he hadn't handed you your lunch at the phony court-martial you had DoD set up, I would have looked like a fool. And you do understand that Bivens has already phoned Santiago and has the full story of what went on in the trial. I think we can beat it back, but what I'm worried about is the full disclosure of Xyze. By the way, where did you come up with that name?" Baron didn't want an answer. "I'm worried that a full disclosure of you and Xyze, the world's finest security concern, buying security from the enemy we are supposed to be fighting won't play well, especially with you making money off the deal. If a definitive link can be made between the money you paid for protection and the Taliban weapons purchases, other than what has come out already, I, and I mean you, have a real problem. There is a lot that I can paper over, but this isn't good."

"I think I have a solution for that, Mr. President." King was grasping.

"Well, it had better be better than the work you've done to date, because honestly, you guys stink." Baron smiled as he got in the dig. "What's your idea?"

"All the bad press is centered around Xyze. What I intend to do is to have ISSAC announce that since Xyze was involved in the massacre, it is being disbanded as a company. We'll throw out a big PR spiel that will make it look like we are punishing those who failed to adhere to the high standards expected of them."

"I thought you told me that Xyze was a big moneymaker."

"It is, and I don't intend to lose the income. What I'll do is shuffle around some of the managers and rename the company. It will allay a lot of problems, and we can conduct business as usual. The Xyze name will be expunged and, along with it, the talk of the massacre and the story about paying the Taliban for protection."

"That's the Erik I know." Baron liked the solution.

"In about three months, we'll rename the security firm a second time, then Xyze will be footnote in history."

"That covers you, but I've got to be able to back out of this looking good." Baron was thinking. "I'm going to lay this off on Stan Weeks. He was the one who sold the idea of a final battle to end the war." Baron had edited from his mind that it was he who had pushed the idea on Weeks. "We'll bury the story of the battle in a rollout. I'll announce that we have made gains in back-channel negotiations with the Taliban and are going into full-on negotiations. I'll make a spectacle of telling the negotiators to be hard, but whatever they come away with will suffice. I don't intend to have them give anything up to get your three guys back." The president floated the idea to see if he still had King's buy-in.

"Consider them collateral damage. We've already taken them off our books." King gave his approval.

"For the next couple of weeks, I'll mention that the negotiations are progressing and that we are winning at the bargaining table. I think that will cover up the reporting that is sure to ferret out that we are being handed our asses in selling out the Afghan government. I don't really care. I want us out of there."

"I like it." King agreed with the president's plan. He had hoped to put Baron in an accepting mood because he had a favor to ask. "There's a loose end that has to be cut off, and I'm going to need your help in getting it done." King eased into his request. "That marine sergeant major and the English reporter still have critical papers that could undo my plans to reorganize Xyze. We have already put a legal hold on the sergeant major's papers, but the Englishman has copies of the amounts of money we spent on our own security. It would be better if those didn't see the light of day. They could cause any number of problems for both you and me. I'd appreciate it if you would intercede with the Brits to stop any more of this story from being published."

"How'd you let these guys get you tied up in knots?" Baron laughed.

"It isn't just me. It would be in both our interests if you could squelch the Englishman's plans. You are, after all, the commander in chief on whose watch this all took place. There could be blowback from this at any time."

"I see what you're saying." Baron thought for a moment. "I'll get everything classified, make everything top secret, so that the English reporter, even if he has access to it, will not be able to use it. Or we'll have the Brits lock him up as a threat to US national security. Can you think of anything else that has to be papered over to put this behind us?"

"No, sir. I think we've covered all the bases. Do you need anything more from me?"

Baron was silent for a moment. "The intelligence rats are hyping up some new kind of disease. I think it's more of their effort to discredit me, so I'd like you to use your sources to find out if there is anything to it."

"I'll get my best people on it and get some answers."

"Erik, you've managed to get into every agency and department in Washington, and now I want you to break into the intelligence cabal. I need people I can trust on the inside of that community. I need people who will work for me instead of against me. You understand what I'm saying?"

"I read you loud and clear, Wil. I've been wanting to privatize the intelligence club for a while, and I have plans for doing it. All I've been waiting for was the okay."

"You have it." Baron was happy, thinking he might get some people loyal to him inside the CIA.

"I'll get it done for you." King was thinking that if he could get his personnel into the intelligence machinery, he would be the most powerful man in government.

The Opening Move